"It will not be hard for a reader to imagine himself living in Cornwall, England, in the time of Queen Elizabeth I, a time when the fear of witches and demons was as real as the dread of storm and shipwreck. . . . The story will especially interest older girls who enjoy a touch of witch-craft in a story." Washington *Star*

". . . the characters are engaging and unpretentious; the atmosphere reeks of pentacles, spells, and brews . . ."
School Library Journal

". . . you feel you have stepped back four centuries into a strange and lovely land." Chicago *Tribune*

White
Witch
of
Kynance

White Witch of Kynance

A Novel by Mary Calhoun

Frontispiece by John Gundelfinger

A HARPER TROPHY BOOK

Harper & Row, Publishers

New York, Evanston, San Francisco, London

To my husband and priest, Leon

I am especially grateful to William Bottrell, Cornish folklorist of the nineteenth century, for his three volumes of *Traditions and Hearthside Stories of West Cornwall*. Bottrell's lively tales form the background for some of this book.

Once a giant lived there. Once in the old days of Cornwall the giant Boclas had sat on that stone and rocked above the sea. A giant—and now she would touch his sacred stone.

Jennet stopped short in her run across the moor, heart pounding as she looked down at the Giant's Castle. Stop, slow, she warned herself. Don't ruin it all. She shouldn't come running, heedless as a chicken, upon this place. Not to this fearful, holy place.

The Castle was almost an island. Here the headland dropped to the shore, then rose again in a rocky spine thrusting out into the sea. Masses of granite surged up from the waves like half-ruined walls, and at the far end, crowning the highest crag, was a great balanced stone, the Logan Rock. There the giant had sat, logging, rocking, taking his ease above the waves.

Jennet's breath came in gasps. She pressed her chest to steady the pounding. *You can reach the Rock. You must.*

For then she could be a witch.

Touch the Logan Rock nine times without moving it, and you can be a witch. Everyone knew that.

To be a white witch—Jennet felt the desire in her so strong it could almost carry her over the rocks by thought. Already she could see herself touching the stone, out there against the sky. Then she would have the power to be a white witch like An Marget, healing wisewoman of the village, Charmer of Kynance. Not a black witch, but a white witch with power over black-ness. Oh, to have the powers of magic against all the fears, the terrible dark things that moved in the empty countryside and stirred at midnight beside one's own hearth. And in one's mind. Remembering, Jennet shrank into herself, clutching her thin arms across her chest.

Her heavy breathing sounded in the silence, and she put up a hand to cover the sound. Nothing moved along the deserted seacoast. Even the gulls were quiet as they stood on the rocks of the Castle. The sun was down, and pink light hazed over the ocean that stretched smooth to the horizon. Waves spuming white against the granite walls only accented the silence. Dusk would come soon, and then the dark.

Now. Now was the time for good to happen. She

could make it happen, if she'd only try. Now, Jennet! she commanded herself. Hampering skirt—she tucked it up to her waist. Black hair falling around her face— she bound it back with a thread. Magic holed stone— yes, it hung at her throat. She began her descent.

The path led down the steep hillside over rock that had worn through, but there was short grass under her feet, too, and little blue spring flowers. Then the sand and pebbles of the shore pricked her feet, and soon she stepped onto the giant's land. Boulders rose above her, heavy brown against the pink light. She ought to call some greeting, a propitiation to the Spirit of the Place . . .

Boclas, Protector of Kynance, he had been. From this sea castle, Boclas had stridden forth to fight the other giants, to protect the village people. The old Kynance giant was a friendly fellow, the tales went, even matching his skill at bowling stones with a certain strong young man from the village who used to come out to visit Boclas in his castle. Now only the spirit of Boclas dwelt in this place—and who knew about spirits? A live giant might be friendly, but once changed to a spirit—?

"Hail!" Jennet called up to the crag of boulders. "Please?"

Her voice was thin, lost in the rush of waves against the rocky base. A gull on a ledge above didn't move its head at her cry.

She had to climb up through the rocks and then out along the ridge to the balanced rock at the end. There was a path. Others had come here, Jennet reminded herself. She started up the path between brown boulders that only a giant could have moved, pulling herself over them as the walls rose. Climbing was no problem. She'd scrambled around many a sea cliff, and her feet were hard from years of running on the moors. Her toes gripped the granite, and she felt strong.

Yet when she climbed onto another boulder and stood up on it and looked down, suddenly she was dizzy. She looked far down at the waves crashing against the jagged rocks, saw herself falling, shrieking . . .

"Fool!" she said fiercely.

Fool, to fear the rocks and waves which she'd always known. Jennet put her head up and walked higher above the sea.

But the Logan Rock loomed impossibly highest upon the tower of stones. The path ended. To reach the Rock she must climb a nearly sheer stone wall. If she slipped—Jennet's hands became cold and damp. Never mind—hurry. The light was fading. It would be even harder to find her way back in the dark.

Her fingers found crevices in the rock face; toes searched for outcroppings. Panting, she pulled herself up. The roaring in her ears blurred out the sound of the waves; her eyes saw only the stone. Arms over the top—she gouged a knee—she stood.

All of the seacoast lay below her, beachless cliffs rising out of the waves, rocky elbows of land wind-bare of trees. The pink light was gone. One pale star showed in the blue sky, and the water lay under it, blue and smooth as the sky except for the edges of the sea that pounded at the rocks below. Returning and returning waves, Jennet thought, returning when the giant had lived here, returning now, returning forever.

It was an easy walk over to the Logan Rock, great round stone balanced on another boulder. It was slightly hollowed on the top where Boclas had sat. Jennet tilted her head as she looked at it. Did it move? It must be her own breathing that had made her eyes move. And a trick of the fading light. Jennet stopped breathing and stared at the Rock. Still it moved. Very slightly, back and forth, it swayed on its balance point. There was no wind . . . The giant! Oh, Lord and all the angels, was the old giant seated there, invisible, rocking in the dusk? Jennet clutched the holed stone at her throat. Something swooped over her head, sudden as a blow, and she screamed and fell to her knees.

The swooping thing was a gull. It landed on the Logan Rock. The white bird stood on the boulder, and as Jennet watched, the creature seemed to move with the sway of the Rock, its beak rising against the sky. The gull—it was the Spirit of the Place, the spirit of Boclas in the gull. She knew it as surely as if she'd seen

5

the giant sitting there. Jennet trembled at its presence. It looked at her and uttered a mewling cry that warned "Stay away!" How dared she presume to use the Giant's Rock, to be a witch?

She lifted a hand and breathed, "Please, I—"

The gull launched toward her, white wings spread —the Spirit was flying to attack her! Jennet's sight went black with fear. She scrambled to the rock face, slid down, scrabbled for holds, then fell to the ground below. Rolling, she clutched a rock just in time to save herself from a last plunge to the waves. She clambered to her feet and darted back along the path, falling down the boulders, while the Spirit flew in circles above her, dipping low, crying at her.

Jennet clung to the magic stone at her throat and gasped over and over, "Oh, Lord! . . . And all the . . . angels!" But God and His angels were far away. The angry Spirit of the Place was here, screaming at her for invading, presuming.

Yet it seemed satisfied with driving her away. When at last she ran down to the shore and reached the mainland, the gull turned and winged out to sea, uttering its cries of triumph. Jennet ran up the cliff path to the moor, her mouth salty with the taste of fear, her heart thudding until she had to drop and gasp for breath. She could barely see the Logan Rock against the dark sky. Something white circled over it, Spirit Triumphant. Always, always the spirits must have their power. The fear—it was like the time—Jennet's eyes blurred, and she looked away from the Rock. She tried not to remember, but the memory came anyway.

She was a child. It was autumn, and she had gone over the moor to play with Nelly Polgrain, who lived alone with her mother. Dark had come on, so Jennet spent the night with the Polgrains, the three of them sleeping in the one bed. In the night, something woke Jennet, something startling, for her heart was pounding even as she came awake. She heard a whispering sound and looked to see what made it. In the last firelight from the hearth she saw movement in the air, writhings, twistings, like smoke trying to take the shape of a figure. Then she saw the shadowed cottage was full of moving shapes that would not form into anything recognizable. The room whispered with them.

In fright, she had reached to Nelly's mother for comfort. But to her horror the body was cold. She had reached over and shaken Nelly awake, crying, "Your mother's dead!"

"No," Nelly had murmured sleepily. "She's not dead. Some nights she goes out of her body."

The whisperings and twistings thickened in the firelight. Jennet tried to cry out and found she couldn't speak. Through the night she lay awake beside the cold body.

She must have slept at last, for she woke again to

see sunlight on the cottage floor and Mistress Polgrain bending to cook at the hearth. Jennet was full of fear at what she might see in the woman's face, and she opened her mouth to scream, but no sound came. She leapt out of the cottage door and ran home. When she got there, they said her mother was dead. Not Nelly's mother—hers! Jennet couldn't speak until the next May, when her grandmother took her to the Holy Well and healing water was put on her throat. She never went back to the Polgrain house, and one night Nelly and her mother were found dead in their bed.

Jennet began to run again. She stumbled up the cliff path in the darkness after one more look at the rocky castle, dark against the sea. She'd failed. It was hard to realize. How could she go on with the rest of her plan? Of course, she'd never known anyone who'd tried to touch the Logan Rock and succeeded. But she'd expected to. The omens had been good. Last autumn she'd caught nine leaves as they fell, and that meant nine months of the next year would be happy ones.

"Wrong!" she cried bitterly.

Life was such a maze when you never knew which omens to believe, when the sayings and rules didn't hold. A person was just at the mercy of the wind, Jennet thought, whether it chose to blow good or evil. Out of a clear summer sky a hailstorm would flash and ruin the crops of a good man. The meanest woman in the village owned the hens that laid the most eggs. What could you rely on in this confused world? It was like feet trying to find sure ground in boggy land, as hard to see your way as it was to see in the dark now.

The blackness of night was complete. Jennet had reached the wasteland that stretched back from the top of the cliff, but she knew it only because furze and brambles scraped her ankles. It was so dark she couldn't see the ups and downs of the ground, and her body jolted with her missteps. She could barely make out the humping line of the moor against the sky.

Jennet tried never to be out after dark, for then the people of blackness came out, spirits that moved over the land in the night, demons, black witches.

At last her feet felt the smooth, packed dirt of the path that led from one village to the next along the coast. She saw a glimmer of light from a cottage high up on the moor. It was almost the only house between here and Kynance Churchtown, and the village lights couldn't be seen because Kynance lay in a valley that ran down to the sea. This was one of the loneliest stretches of the north coast of West Cornwall. Once Jennet had traveled the twenty miles to St. Ives, and the light at night in the market town had stunned her. There were so many houses and shops letting out their candlelight that she could see where she walked in any street. On the south coast too, she had heard that the villages and farms beyond Penzance were so close together you were hardly ever beyond the sight of a cottage light at night.

Oh well, the south coast was soft. That's what everyone said. It was soft living there, with all the trees and green fields and chatter of people. We're stronger, Jennet thought. They had to be, here on the barren north coast, clearing rocks to farm the wasteland, fighting the sea for fish. Jennet tried to feel proud and strong in the dark, but her hand went up to the stone at her neck, and when she put her little finger through the hole, she felt helpless instead. Even the magic stone had failed to protect her.

Once her grandmother—dead now—had said that a stone with a hole in it was powerful magic against evil because such stones were made by the fairy people, the piskies. Jennet had found the little rock one day on the shore. That time in St. Ives when she'd goggled at all the people in the marketplace, she'd seen a man in gray robes. He was a turned-out monk, someone had whispered to her. Over his robe had hung a wooden cross. She wondered if it gave him any more protection than her stone did. It hadn't saved him from being turned out. Of course, Pastor Thomas would fuss if anyone in the village tried to wear a cross, anyway. Jennet laughed suddenly. Ha, if he knew she wore a magic stone! Little she cared what Piggy Thomas thought.

A stone structure bulked in the darkness, and Jennet quieted. This was Boclas Quoit, the burial dolmen of the old giant. Three great stones stood upright, with a flat capstone on top of them. Here the dying giant had sat, looking out over the ocean while his friend, the young man from the village, had piled the burial carn around him. That's the way the story went. And all so long ago that not even the giant's bones remained. The dolmen stood high enough for Jennet to walk under it—not that she had a mind to. She could barely make out the shape of the ancient cromlech in the darkness, and she hurried her steps past it, watching it warily.

—Oh, Lord, what moved?

A figure moved beside the stones. Jennet screamed and ran, stumbling, crying. The figure dashed after her, caught her by the shoulders.

"Oh no oh no oh no!" Jennet babbled.

"Jennet! Jennet Trevail! It's only me. It's all right."

Jennet twisted out of the grasp. Faces so close, she saw a blessed, solid human, a young man. It was Robin Pender. He was carrying a sack, and he was laughing. Relief was so sharp she broke into laughter with him, laughter still close to screaming. She sank down on the path.

"I thought you were the Dark Master!" she gasped.

Yet she felt a hot thrill run through her. Had it been, she could only have surrendered, and the struggle would now be over. There was a tale of a girl who had been overtaken on the moor by the Dark Huntsman and his hounds one night. He had carried her away to an orchard of sweet evil. But, Jennet remembered, the girl had returned the next day an old woman. No, she didn't want that.

Robin was laughing at her words, and Jennet relaxed at the good sound in the darkness. Robin Pender was a merry lad, and Kynance folk were beginning to call him Rob-Bob in acceptance. Jennet hadn't seen him often, for he was of the Pender clan who lived at Penmorvah, the next village out the coast. He had just come over to Kynance last winter to work the farm of his ailing aunt, Sarah Pender.

"Aye, I can believe the Dark Master would want you," Robin said, chuckling.

Jennet chilled. "Why?"

"For your beauty, lass!"

He reached down and pulled her up to walk on along the footpath. In embarrassment, she saw that her skirt was still tucked up to her waist, and she jerked it down. She didn't know what to say. She wasn't used to the banter of courting lads.

"And what are you doing, couranting in the hills after dark? Meeting a friend?" he went on teasing her. "Yes, miss, I heard you laugh. Just before you saw me."

All the fear and stress—her mind was too confused to settle down to light talk. She began a hasty answer.

"I was laughing at Piggy Thomas—Pastor Thomas —oh, he's not here—I mean—"

12

His face was turned toward her. She couldn't see his expression, but his voice was gentle. "Never mind," he said.

She liked the gentleness of his voice. Yet it made her feel like a foolish child, being humored. Really, it was all his fault, scaring her like that by the dolmen.

She countered, "And what are you doing out so late, sir? What's in your sack? I think I've caught you at free-trading." Along the coast, there was always a bit of smuggling going on.

"Ho!" Robin said. "Hard times if we must smuggle in rabbits now!" He slung the sack off his back and shook it in front of her. "I've been out emptying my snares. Tonight we'll eat rabbit pie instead of fish, An Sarah and I."

"Oh."

Jennet couldn't think of anything else to say. She looked up at the tall young man walking beside her, and puzzled how to talk to him.

"Your face is white as the moon," he said, looking down. "Strange how it glows soft in the dark. Have you ever seen your face, Mistress Jennet?"

Jennet looked away. He was teasing her again. Yes, she'd seen her face. Amongst her dead mother's things had been a piece of polished tin, which now hung on the wall of the cottage. Her sisters and Molly, her stepmother, were always studying themselves in the shining round. Jennet looked only occasionally—to see who she was. She didn't have the broad cheekbones of most of the Kynance girls. Hers was a thin face with a pointed chin. Her eyes were set wide, and if the tin reflected truly, their gray-blue was almost black at the outer rims. The last time she'd looked, she'd caught her breath because she couldn't see the tiny image of herself reflected in the pupil. If you can't see yourself reflected in another person's eyes, that person is bewitched. She'd run to her older sister, begging "Can you see yourself in my eyes?" At first Nancy had peered and teased, "No." But then she'd said, "Oh, of course I can, silly."

Anyway, she knew what a scared, narrow face she had. "Stop teasing about my face, Robin Pender," she said, her voice sharp. "I know what I look like."

"Very well," he said cheerfully. "I leave you here anyway. Go well, Jennet. May you laugh with God."

And he was gone, leaping up the hill towards An Sarah's cottage. Jennet tried to see after him in the darkness. Well! He needn't have left so suddenly. Her sharp, awkward way must have disgusted him. He'd not spare a glance for her face again. And he was such a good, laughing Rob-Bob, a man of sunlight. "May you laugh with God." What kind of a god laughed? She didn't laugh easily when she was teased, the way her sisters did. She wished she could laugh the way Robin did. Her beauty, he'd said. Could he have meant it?

Jennet stamped her foot fiercely. "Stop that!" she

told herself. She had no business mooning after lads. She was going to be a white witch with power to protect herself, not depend on some feeble human man to keep the dark spirits away. Instead of a housewife, she'd be a powerful wisewoman, the most important woman in the village. Jennet willed her thoughts away from Robin to An Marget.

Over and over she'd planned it: She'd touch the Logan Rock. Then, with assurance, she'd go to An Marget and tell that she'd been given the power to be a witch. She'd beg to be taken on as an apprentice to the white witch. In return, she'd be An Marget's serving girl for as long as the woman liked. In the service of the Charmer of Kynance she'd learn how to heal with herbs, she'd learn the charms, she'd become wise. And at last she'd be able to banish the demon that had come to possess her.

She'd clung to the hope for a long time, trying to gain courage to take the step. Then this week Nancy had forced it. Nan had told that she and her Will would be wed before summer—and Jennet was nearly as old as Nancy. That meant she'd have to leave her father's crowded house soon too. They'd expect her to marry, or else seek work as a serving girl at one of the rich farms in the lowlands, over the moors to the south.

Well, she wouldn't go that helpless way. She'd learn Marget's power over darkness.

But now how could she? She hadn't touched the

Rock. Without that to tell, why would Marget consent to take her on? Jennet had never spoken to the old woman. An Marget lived apart, a remote, awesome person. She was called "An," but all old women were called "Aunt," just as all old men were "Uncle." Marget was aunt to no one in the village. Nobody seemed to know her surname or much about her past history, but there were tales.

Margaret had appeared in Kynance many years before, riding a horse, a bag of gold tied to the saddle. They said she might have come from one of the great families on the south coast. With her gold, she had commanded a stone cottage to be built out on a cliff by the sea. The village of Kynance straggled up the valley into a sheltered place between the hills, where a few big trees grew and the mill stood on the stream. But An Marget's house sat alone, out on the cliffs, yet tucked in a fold that protected her from the wind. She called the place Chelew, which in the Cornish language meant "sheltered house." The tales went that she had waited patiently while the granite rocks were gathered from the fields, while the village mason had laid up the stone walls and chinked them with clay. And she had made him build her shadow into the walls.

"It shall be my strong house, and no one can take it from me," she had said.

She was right. Who'd try to dwell in a house with a witch's shadow built into it?

There An Marget lived, in a corner out of the wind that came up the valley from the sea. She'd planted an herb garden to heal folk, but she'd never mingled with the village. The people had to come to her. She didn't live alone though, for she had many animals. People told of seeing her walking on the cliffs with her pet goats and lambs. Those who had run to her for help told of the tame hares that wandered into her cottage to rest by the hearth, of a cat that perched on the windowsill, a magpie that screeched on the roof, poultry that clucked in the dooryard. They said robins and wrens flew in the open windows to nest under the thatch of the roof, and a swarm of bees had hung a honeycomb from the rafters, so birds flitted and twittered and bees hummed along with An Marget's spinning wheel. Yet with all the beasts, people said everything indoors was as clean and sweet as the roses and thyme in her garden.

Jennet had walked nearly to the village. Lights glimmered through the shutters of a few of the houses. Soon she'd come to the lane that led up to the Trevail cottage, but here was the track that wandered off toward the sea cliffs and An Marget's house. Which way? The Spirit of the Place had denied her. Yet if she didn't take Marget's path now, she'd go home and nothing would ever change. Jennet pressed her hands against her neck, ran them back under her lop of hair, and stared into the darkness. She had to go to An

Marget. There was no other way. Jennet turned onto the white witch's path.

I'll find out what to say when I get there, she told herself.

Although the wind buffeted this coast almost unceasingly, there was no wind now, and the night was strangely soft, with a haze in the air. As Jennet neared the cottage she smelled the sharp tang of some herb and the sweetness of a night-blooming flower. In the daytime Jennet had crept around these cliffs, watching for a glimpse of the old woman and studying the cottage, but she'd never been in the house. Not that she could remember. She wondered if her grandmother had brought her to Marget when she couldn't speak. Perhaps it had been the wisewoman who had advised taking her to the Holy Well up over the moors.

A bit of light showed through a shutter. Jennet glanced around the dooryard, nervous that she might step on some stray animal, but none seemed to be about. She stepped to the closed door. What—what would she say? Now, ready— She lifted her hand to knock. And stopped. She heard voices inside. Someone was with An Marget.

Jennet clutched her arms across her chest impatiently. She couldn't wait. She might lose courage—

The voices murmured. One was a deep voice. What went on in a witch's house at night? Someone must have come for help. Was An Marget chanting a spell?

I don't want to see it. One foot stepped out to run. Then her eyes narrowed. *Yes, I do.*

Jennet walked softly to the window shutter with its slit of light and put her eye to the crack. Her breath sighed out. No scene of witchcraft here. Instead, she saw two people visiting by the fireplace, as cozy and ordinary as in any cottage in West Cornwall—though the cottage was furnished a bit better than the ordinary Kynance hut. On the shelf over the fire, pewter and brass gleamed softly in the candlelight. In one corner stood a tall cupboard of shelves and drawers, made of oak and handsomely carved. And An Marget sat in a real chair, a high-backed oak chair, polished and carved.

Certainly the white witch looked like no ordinary countrywoman, even sitting at her knitting by the hearth. Jennet had seen her strong, confident face at a distance outdoors, but now in the firelight An Marget's face seemed to show its real being. The flickering light emphasized her features, throwing a shadow along her hawklike nose, making deep places of her eyes, carving the strong lines that were not the usual crumpling of wrinkles. An Marget was old, probably near fifty, yet the hair at her forehead under her scarf was a glossy reddish-black.

Settled on a bench opposite her was a wide-chested old man, his short legs propped up on a stool. He was Uncle Mathy Curnow. Of course, everyone in the village knew Uncle Mathy—Captain Mathy. He was a graybeard, but he had a hearty red face, roughed from being out in all weather. Jennet remembered then that people said he was an old friend of Marget's, the only friend she accepted. Uncle Mathy had a field and a few cows near Kynance, but most of the time he left the farm in the care of his wife and boys. He liked to spend his time at streaming tin up on the moor, where he was captain of a crew of men he'd gathered. They had a comfortable moor house by the stream, where they'd drink and trade tales at night, and the village said it was a shame how Uncle Mathy often stayed away all week, leaving poor Jone to work the farm. No one scolded Mathy Curnow to his face though. He was a blustery fellow, good in a fight.

Besides, Jennet thought, you couldn't help liking him. He was a chatty old man, too, and he told a good tale. He could have made a living as a wandering droll-teller. Jennet listened now in hopes of a story, but he seemed to have just finished one, for he and An Marget burst into laughter.

". . . so he kicked the cow!" Uncle Mathy repeated, reaching over to slap her knee. He rocked with chuckles at his tale, and An Marget's white teeth flashed as she laughed.

"Oh, Mathy, I'm glad you've come! You're the only one who makes me laugh," she said. But her face sobered and shadowed under the scarf as she added, "We Cornish can imagine anything. Yet for all of it, we're a humorless lot. In the village—the people—their idea of a joke is a cruel trick."

"Now, Marget, don't be getting wisht," Uncle Mathy said easily, leaning back on the settle. "Here now, what do you think of this? They say Queen Elizabeth might come to Cornwall." He sipped from a mug on the bench beside him.

An Marget looked down at her knitting. "Why would she want to do that?"

Jennet had tilted her head at the sound of the woman's voice. For all the Charmer's fame, Jennet had never heard her speak until tonight. Her words seemed too ordinary for such a voice. It had a husky, rich-colored sound, and then at its bottom was a level like base rock.

"Perhaps to consult you, old dear!" Uncle Mathy laughed.

The woman glanced up, and her dark eyes sparked with the firelight. Jennet couldn't read her look.

Jennet had heard of a queen called Elizabeth, but she and England were as far away as a queen in fairyland. Queen Elizabeth might come riding a unicorn, for all Jennet knew. Yet Elizabeth and England ruled Cornwall. When a Cornishman said "England," he spat. Still, Jennet had heard some of the village men say grudgingly that Elizabeth might be all right. It was said she liked sailors, and the Cornish were men of the sea. Even though they farmed or dug for tin, at some time or other the men sailed out to fish, to smuggle in a bit of contraband goods, or to seek their fortunes at raiding Spanish ships.

Uncle Mathy's voice rose angrily, and Jennet listened again. The talk had changed. It seemed that he'd come to consult the wisewoman on business, after all.

"My cows are ill-wished," he was insisting, thumping his mug on the settle. "The poor things are thin and starved, no matter how much they eat, and they're covered with sores."

"No wonder—" An Marget started to say, but Uncle Mathy went on roughly.

"Someone has ill-wished them in the evil moment so that the curse didn't fall harmless to the ground!"

"Nay, you old fool!" An Marget retorted. "It's your own fault. It's a wonder to me those young cows aren't ill-wished every hour of the day, for they're breachy as goats. If you'd stay home and mend your hedges, they'd stay out of other people's fields."

Jennet almost laughed to see An Marget scold the bluster out of the old man. She said he neglected his pastures. If he'd dress them with seaweed and sand as others did, enough grass would grow to feed the poor cows. Uncle Mathy shook his head and puffed out his beard, but he sat smaller on the settle. When he spoke again, his voice was timid.

"Well, but Margaret, the cows—they're still thin,

even though they eat in other folk's pastures."

The woman bent her head over her work and knit several stitches. As Jennet watched her, she saw a strange look ripple over Marget's face, leaving it harder. The jaw jutted, and a shadow lay black along her hawk nose.

"Very well," she said, looking straight at Mathy. "I will help you find the ill-wisher."

She sprang up from her chair, her movements as strong as a young woman's, and went to the oak cupboard. Taking out an earthen jar, she said, "This bottle holds magic water. Bury it with these words." She handed the jar to Mathy and murmured something into his ear. "Then the person who ill-wished your cattle will begin to feel pain and confess. But don't cork the bottle too tightly, for fear of what might happen."

Jennet drew in her breath. There'd be trouble now. She wished she could have heard the white witch's charm.

Uncle Mathy only seemed happy to see the business go so well. He got up, chuckling, saying, "Thankee, old friend! I'll bring more furze for your fire, for I see your rick is getting low."

She replied, "I wish you well till I see you again, Mathy," seeing him out the door.

Jennet crouched back in the darkness along the cottage wall. The woman remained in the lit doorway until Matthew Curnow had gone into the dark on the path towards Kynance.

Then An Marget called in a sharp whisper, "I know someone's near. Come out!"

Jennet wasn't surprised that the witch could sense her presence, but she was ashamed to be caught slinking like a thief. This was a bad start. She came from behind a bush, smoothing down her skirt, and ducked a quick curtsy.

"Mistress Margaret, I came to tell you—" she began. Tell what? Quick, what should she say? "Tonight I went to the Logan Rock!" she blurted.

She couldn't see the woman's face. It was in shadow, with the firelight coming from behind her. Instead, Marget studied Jennet in the faint light.

"You climbed all the way up to it?"

Jennet nodded. Everyone knew how dangerous the path was.

Slowly An Marget said, "I think you are a very—"

Jennet waited to hear "brave."

"—silly girl." She thrust her head forward. "Come now, what do you want?"

Jennet's whole body flushed with heat. After all this, to be made fun of!

Furious, she cried, "I want to be a witch!"

The woman only laughed softly. "You want to dabble in the black arts?" she teased. "Come, girl, was it a love potion you were wanting?"

To Marget she was just a silly country girl. Why should the Charmer of Kynance bother with her? Jennet began, "I—" and a sob choked out of her. Between sobs she cried, "I want to work for you—learn to be a white witch—protect myself from the demon!" She dropped her face into her hands and sagged.

Through her sobs she heard Marget say, "Poor girl." The richness of the voice soothed her; even the hard base to it was reassuring. She felt Marget take one of her hands from her face.

"We all fear the dark," the old woman said. "Do you see that?"

Jennet started. Something white moved near her feet. Then she saw it was only a chicken.

"Here, Biddy." An Marget clucked her tongue at the hen, and it answered with a soft *cluttering*. "You see, girl, not a ghost in the night, only a sleepy hen."

Jennet looked at the harmless chicken. Good sense, of course, but—

"I have seen spirits!" she said harshly. "Did my grandmother bring me to you?"

In a tumble of words she told of the night she'd lain next to Mistress Polgrain's cold body. How her mother had died on the night the spirits came. Telling, she began to tremble and to cry again. No use. No hope, ever . . . And she hated the sound of her sobs in the still night outside the cottage. She gasped back the sound and turned to hunt the path to Kynance.

How do you expect to see, she thought angrily, with your eyes full of tears?

"I think I can use you."

Jennet stopped with her back to the voice. She whirled.

"Yes? Oh, I'll work, I'll work for you—"

The woman was already moving back through the doorway. "Come tomorrow morning," she said and closed the door.

2

Elbows and knees poked into Jennet, and a warm back pressed against her side. She woke slowly the next morning, thinking, We Trevails sleep like a litter of cats. Last night she'd had a glimpse of An Marget's handsome oak bed up on the talfat, a whole bed for just one person. All of the Trevails slept on the talfat, the stage built halfway out over the room and reached by a ladder. Jan Trevail and his second wife, Molly, lay in a slightly raised frame for their straw mattress. Scattered around them in the straw on the talfat floor were Nancy, Jennet, and Loveday, Jan's daughters by his first wife, and Jemmy and Dick, Moll's sons.

But it was a warm way to sleep. Jennet found a more comfortable position in the huddle, and her mouth curled. Apprenticed for a witch! Now there'd be the excitement of spells and charms to learn, dramatic scenes in the white witch's cottage when people came for help, the mysteries, and at last—the knowledge she needed. A new and wonderful life—and she'd reached out and taken it for herself. By her own power.

By deceiving? Jennet squirmed suddenly. She'd let An Marget think she'd touched the Logan Rock. Jennet raised up on one elbow and stared into the smoky gloom of the cottage. She wondered how much An Marget knew without being told. Slyness—it made a bad beginning. Especially if the wisewoman knew her apprentice was pretending a lie.

I'll have to tell her the truth, Jennet thought in dismay. Oh, she couldn't. Then Marget might send her away—the end before there was ever a beginning.

But maybe not. The old woman hadn't seemed impressed by her deed of going to the Logan Rock. They'd talked a long time after she'd told that. And then Jennet wondered, why *had* An Marget accepted her? Right at the end she'd changed—"I can use you." Jennet sat up from the swarm of bodies, puzzled, uneasy, trying to remember the conversation. At last she shrugged. She'd have to tell the truth. What happened then was in An Marget's hands.

Moving cautiously, she untangled herself from the sleepers, to hurry off to Chelew before anyone woke to detain her. But Jemmy, the youngest, felt her easing away. Immediately he grabbed her ankle and cried for his breakfast. That woke Dick, and he grabbed her other ankle. She whispered and cuffed at them and couldn't help laughing until her sisters protested, and it ended with Jennet being pushed below to stir up the fire and cut the bread.

Jennet hurried. Maybe she still could get away before they all came down. She opened the window shutter to let the stale smoke out, and welcome morning light came into the cottage. How barren it looked compared to Chelew, where the carved oak and polished pewter gleamed in the firelight, and the floor was laid with slabs of slate. The Trevail cottage was only one room with a deep fireplace in the back wall. The floor was nothing but trodden earth—mud in wet weather—and the only furnishings were a rough table, a few stools, a few shelves for the bowls and mugs, a chest, and the women's spinning wheels. Her father made a poor living as a tin miner, and no one would be very sorry when Nancy left to wed. One less mouth to feed, one less person trying for a place by the fire.

Jemmy and Dick were lying on their stomachs, watching her over the edge of the talfat and whispering to her. They were like birds in a nest, with their open mouths. Jennet reached up to poke hunks of bread into their beaks.

"Here. Now hush!"

But just as she turned to the door, there was a knock on it.

"Drat!" she whispered, unbarring the door.

She stopped with her hand on the wooden bolt. A picture flashed into her mind. She saw a woman lying on a bed, and the woman was dead.

Slowly she opened the door, and then the picture disappeared as she caught her breath. Outside in the early morning wind stood Robin Pender, looking at her. His eyes were green. She hadn't been able to see that last night. Vivid green eyes in a tan face, with fair hair curling around his ears—a tawny man. From now on, every yellow-haired man with blue eyes would seem pale.

"She's dead!" he said. "Last night when I got home An Sarah seemed asleep in her bed, so I didn't bother her. But this morning I can't wake her!"

Jennet wasn't surprised. It was a trick of the demon to show her the pictures in other people's minds. But she was too aware of the man in the doorway to be distressed about the demon. Tears stood in Robin's eyes, making the green sparkle. He cared about his crotchety old aunt, Jennet thought. Everyone else called her the stingiest woman around. None of the Pender clan except Robin had offered to help on her little farm when she fell sick.

"I'm sorry." Jennet reached out a hand to touch his shoulder, then jerked it back. "What can I— Come in."

"You'd help," he said, smiling at her. He stepped inside.

Actually he'd come to fetch Molly Trevail. She was the one who laid out the bodies for the village and sat with the dead when the family women couldn't. The dead didn't scare her, Moll would say, shrugging, and she knew all the things to do before the funeral.

The Trevails came climbing down the ladder to see what the early stir was about. Lovey was younger than Jennet, but she began smoothing her hair and dimpling at the sight of a man. However, Rob followed Jennet to take the mug of ale she had offered him. Jan Trevail only clapped Robin on the shoulder and nodded, then turned to gulp some bread and cheese before he set out on his long walk up the coast to the underground tin mine beyond Penmorvah. Moll and Nancy and Lovey chattered at Robin, though, and he was caught up in talking with them while Jennet stood off at the side, watching.

Molly was soon ready to go with Robin. Abruptly she said, "Jen, come with me. You might as well learn this business. Time you learned something besides running the moors."

"No!" The word startled out of her. Then she laughed. Why, it was almost funny. Expect her to help with the dead? Willingly go where the demons might be gathering this very minute to carry off the soul? Moll certainly didn't know her. Her laughter sounded like sobs. She saw Robin looking at her, puzzled, and she broke off.

"I'm sorry. It's not what you think—I can't—"

"Don't mind her," Molly said. "She's crazy."

Yet Robin urged, "Please come. I'd like for you to be there."

When he smiled, sun-squint lines crinkled around his eyes. There was such a very maleness to his face, his strong body . . . Stop! She looked down.

"No," she said, "I can't."

He turned away, and they left, Moll taking Lovey with her instead. It was natural enough, Jennet thought, for Molly and Loveday were two of a kind—both empty-headed, take-it-day-by-day creatures. Lovey didn't remember any other mother, and there was nothing she and Moll liked better than a good gossip as they sat spinning. Jennet watched Lovey walk away at Robin Pender's side, smiling up at him, flirting already.

Nancy was watching too. "You *are* crazy, Jennet," she scolded. "He wanted you. Now Lovey will get to comfort him in his sadness. And she's too young to wed, despite all her smirking at the boys."

Nancy stood by Jennet in the doorway, and Jennet leaned against her for a moment as Nancy slipped an arm around her. Nancy was tall, with smooth brown hair, and she always looked neat, even now when she'd just come from bed. However, Jennet pulled away from her when Nancy went on fussing about how rich Robin would be since surely he'd inherit An Sarah's farm and money. Nancy was still talking as Jennet ran down the path.

"Yes, you're right!" she called back. "Good-bye!"

Robin Pender! Until last night she'd never given him a thought. Now she kept seeing a certain golden curl under his ear and the way his green eyes had sparkled at her through the tears. And the way he'd kept looking at her. He'd hardly looked at anyone else in the cottage, for all their chatter. But now, Lovey— and if he knew of her pact with An Marget . . . No! She wouldn't be caught up in this courting foolishness and the drab life that followed it—early wed, early bedded, early dead.

As Jennet ran down the path to the village, Kynance Churchtown—thrown down in the valley like a handful of gray pebbles—looked of little importance compared to the wide hills and the sky. The sky was an intimate part of Jennet's world. Often the sky brooded low and gray, like damp, glistening pewter. Clouds swept in from the ocean, bringing sudden violent storms of thunder and lightning. Even on sunny days the sky was not far off, for the moisture in the air brought the blueness cupping just over the hills.

High tors rose inland behind Kynance, great uncultivated hills bristling with rocks and crowned with formations of giant boulders. Closer to the village, the folds of hills were covered with pastures and fields as the land ran down to the sea. Few trees grew on this barren coast—only clumps of wind-shaped oak and beech crouching against the sides of meadows, and a taller growth of trees around the mill back up the stream between the hills.

Kynance itself was a treeless, drab huddle of gray cottages and muddy lanes. The houses were built of earth, or of the gray granite strewn over the hills, and they were all oblong boxes with slanting roofs of thatch. There was a public inn of sorts, but only the square Norman tower of Kynance Church rose above the cottages. Yet it was a sturdy, stocky tower, not a soaring one, and even the granite church seemed to haunch down against the Atlantic gales that could sweep up the valley.

Jennet wasted few glances on gray Kynance when the countryside beyond was bright with April color. The cultivated fields were a green patchwork flung over the hills, for each field was marked off with old stone hedges. The hilly pastures billowed with misty green-ness, as if about to burst and shower out something, perhaps a spatter of flowers. Yellow gorse glowed against the hedge walls, and blue flowers bloomed amongst the ivy that grew over the stone. Even the barren tors behind her flared with patches of golden gorse. And in front of her the blue sea sparkled, ruffed by the wind.

As Jennet took the path to the cliffs, a small bird fluttered up, like a black-and-white butterfly, and uttered a quick, sweet warble. Expertly Jennet whistled an answer to the wheatear's call. Then she began to sing a bouncing song about "Maids and lads, and hey nonny-o!" If she couldn't laugh much, at least singing was the next best thing to laughing.

She stopped singing though when she came near An Marget's house, and her throat was tight again. Once she told what had happened at the Logan Rock, she might find herself going right back to Kynance.

Jennet came out of the wind, down into the fold of the cliff where the witch's house sat. The place was as sunny now as it had been dark last night, and she saw no more mysterious scene than she had then. The old woman was on her knees working in the herb garden beside the cottage. A gray cat leaned against her side, and a magpie stood on the low stone wall above her. Two little apple trees that An Marget had managed to grow under the shoulder of the cliff rustled softly at a corner of the garden. The only thing unusual was that An Marget was talking to the magpie—and the magpie was answering her.

"Who can grow parsley?" she asked.

"Only the wicked," replied the bird. "Only the wicked can grow parsley." Its voice was low and human, yet hollow, without inflection.

Jennet stopped short. An Marget saw her and laughed. "Don't run. As you're to work for me, I'll tell you a secret."

Jennet teetered on the rock where she'd stopped. A witch's secret already, here in the sunlight. Suddenly the whole scheme was frightening. How could she learn to be a witch? Her feet jerked as if to run, but the old woman went on talking.

"That's my pet magpie. I taught him to talk. Let those who will, think him magic." She chuckled. "His name is Malachai."

Jennet saw nothing funny. She stared at the gaudy black-and-white bird with its iridescent blue wings and long tail.

She breathed, "He is your familiar?"

An Marget glanced at her and stopped smiling. Brusquely she said, "He's not of the Devil, if that's what you mean."

Jennet saw that the woman was displeased with her. And there was worse to come.

"I have to tell you," she blurted. "I didn't touch the Logan Rock. I climbed right to it, but the Spirit of the Place wouldn't let me!"

Margaret stood up and walked over to Jennet. Her face was expressionless. "Tell me."

"The Rock moved—the Spirit—there was a gull—" As Jennet tried to tell about it, her hands fluttered, touched her face; she chewed a fingernail.

When she was done, the woman stood silent. The sun was at An Marget's back, and Jennet couldn't see into her eyes, shadowed by her head shawl.

"Spirits . . ." Marget said. Then she shrugged. "Probably a gull only." She paused again before she said, "I've never touched the Logan Rock." She turned toward the garden. "Here, see what you can do with this parsley."

Jennet stared at Marget's back. Was An Marget accepting her? Parsley . . . "only the wicked . . ." Was it a test of her wickedness?

The woman glanced back at her impatiently. "Do you want to work for me?" she said.

Jennet nodded.

"Then come here. Loosen the dirt around these seedlings. Parsley is too weak to come through crusty soil."

The day was devoted to gardening. An Marget showed Jennet how to rake the dirt with her fingers so as not to harm the green sprouts coming through. Jennet set to work on her knees beside the woman, crumbling dirt in the parsley bed. The magpie, however, was furious at her intrusion. It hopped on the wall and screeched in a scolding clack that scraped the ears, and Jennet kept looking up at it apprehensively, for fear that more words would emerge from its chatter. She'd seen plenty of magpies in the hills, and she knew a raven that she thought of as a pet, but it didn't talk. At last An Marget said, "Give over now, Malachai." The bird subsided into gurgles, suddenly said "Heigh-ho!" and flew away.

The quiet was welcome. The gray cat lay under a bush and purred while the women worked in the garden. An Marget didn't speak, and Jennet was too much in awe of her to start conversation. Here she was, actually working with the white witch. But gardening—it was such a homely occupation compared to what she'd expected.

Once Margaret asked, "Do you know gardening?"

Jennet shook her head.

"Hmph!"

She kept Jennet busy all morning, loosening dirt around the rose bushes with a strong forked stick, pulling weeds among the mint. Jennet was soon hot at her work in the sheltered garden, and the old woman offered her no rest or drink of water. Jennet wiped away the sweat that ran down into her eyes, and dug diligently. Probably she was being tested. The woman pointed out a growth of sage that had sprung up by the stones at the bottom of the wall, and she showed her how to plant the sprouts among the marjoram, for "sage likes to grow with marjoram." Then she went into the house and left Jennet to the task.

The sun stood at noonday. An Marget must have gone in to eat. Jennet wished she'd thought to bring along some bread and cheese. However, she found she enjoyed working in the sunny garden. The hill beside the house muffled the sound of the waves and wind beyond, and here it was so quiet she could hear the buzzing of the bees. Jennet liked the rich smell of upturned earth and the feel of the gentle curlings of roots in her fingers. As she dug up and then planted the sage, she began to hum.

"Grow, little sagelings," she sang softly, then changed to a rollicking tune, making up words about growing and "here's to the health of the sage-o!"

"That ought to wake up the lazy plants."

An Marget stood over her, smiling. Jennet laughed. Now here was something to laugh about, singing to plants.

Yet the woman said seriously, "I talk to the plants, to help them grow. Singing should be even better."

Jennet felt even more uncertain about how to behave with the woman when Marget took her into the house. She'd set out a good meal of bread and honey, boiled eggs, cheese, and ale—more food than the Trevails ever had at one meal—and she expected her serving girl to sit down to eat with her. Jennet plopped onto a stool. Then she was embarrassed when An Marget said, "Better wash first." Jennet became aware of the earth on her hands and skirt, of how dirty she was in this neat cottage with its clean-brushed slate floor and the pewter shining on the shelf. At home, where every drop of water had to be carried up from the stream, there was little talk of washing.

But An Marget said briskly, "Plenty of water here, with a spring just beyond the door."

She indicated the bucket of water in the corner and even gave Jennet a soft white towel.

When they had finished eating, An Marget said, "Now, girl, tell me what you know about healing."

Jennet licked the honey from her fingers and wiped them surreptitiously on her skirt. She tried to remember the bits of knowledge she'd picked up. Of course, everyone knew to rub a dock leaf on a nettle sting. She recited:

> *Nettle out, dock in,*
> *Dock remove the nettle sting.*

Sores could be cured, too, by laying fresh-washed dock leaves on them. And the dried powder of a puffball would stop bleeding. When Jemmy and Dick cut themselves as they played, she'd dust this powder into the cuts.

Whilks, the little gatherings on the boys' eyelids—those could be cured by passing a black cat's tail nine times over the places.

An Marget smiled. "Does that work?"

"Of course!" The whilks had always gone away in a few days.

"All right, girl." An Marget cut the recital short. She leaned forward. "Now learn this first: A white witch's art is the art of brewing simples. Herbs, plants, those are my tools. Come outdoors."

With the gray cat leading the way through the

garden, smoothing her tail against the plants as if to emphasize her mistress' words, An Marget taught Jennet the names of the herbs and their values. Jennet strained to memorize her words, for she didn't think the woman would repeat herself.

These were the allheals, angelica and valerian. Valerian, whose tops would flower into purple cushions, was especially good for colic and gripe. Here were thyme, rosemary, and sage. Sage eaten in May ensured old age. This was the adam-and-eve plant, for love potions. Over here were strong-smelling clumps of pennyroyal, rue, and the lemon-scented vervain, to which the cat touched her nose. There were the homely garlic and endive, and there were wild plants, foxglove and sea poppy, which An Marget had moved into the garden. There were stalks of wolfsbane growing in a damp place. Jennet looked at the harmless-looking leaves, wondering.

An Marget said, "Yes, it's dangerous. It can poison. It can heal as well." She snorted. "And when drunken old women use it, their arms tingle, they think they can fly, and they call themselves witches."

Wolfsbane was a wondrous herb, she said. Its power lay not in the tiny blue flowers shaped like a monk's hood, that would climb its stalk, but in the root. Brewed and applied in a poultice, wolfsbane would produce tingling, warmth, and numbness. It could soothe the pain of aching teeth and rheumatic bones.

The tour ended. Jennet looked around the sheltered garden. Sun and shade, rustle of leaves. "Soothe the pain" . . . soothe . . . the echo soothed her toward sleepy content. Humming of bees, purring of cat . . . Jennet looked at An Marget. In the sunlight her face was strong but plain, with no shadows about her angled nose. Jennet could see into her hazel eyes. The Charmer of Kynance bent to smooth her cat. Just like any simple peasant woman in her garden. Just a nice old medicine woman.

Betrayed! Rage exploded in Jennet. Its heat rushed through her body, and she flung out her arms as if to seize the crouching woman.

"Is this all?" she demanded. "What about the spells and the charms? What about the spirits? The power!"

An Marget rose up swiftly. Her eyes pierced like spears. Her look bore into Jennet, and Jennet shrank back. How could she have . . . She firmed herself. She'd come in faith.

Marget's face was grim as a gray sea. Then the lines around her eyes softened, and she laughed suddenly, a shout.

"Challenge!" she exclaimed. "No milksop girl here. Aye, Jennet, you'll do."

Jennet waited for her answer. She looked at the woman's eyes; the brown-flecked eyes looked back at her. Honest eyes, meeting, answering . . .

"Yes, there is power," An Marget said. "There are

42

spells and charms—and twists in people. I will teach you how to sort out the nonsense." She paused. "Spirits?"

Her head bowed, and the meeting of eyes was broken. Her head shawl stood out around her face, shadowing it. Jennet had the feeling that the woman had stepped back into a cave. When she spoke again, it was as if to herself.

"Yes, there are mysteries."

There was silence in the garden. The magpie flew across it with a soft swish of wings and landed on the wall.

"Come back tomorrow," Marget said.

An Marget? In the days that followed, Jennet was fascinated with her lessons in white witchcraft, but she was even more intrigued by the puzzle of the woman. When she'd planned to apprentice herself to the Charmer, Marget had been only a figure who could release knowledge. She hadn't thought about working daily with a real person.

At home she'd said only that she was going to be An Marget's serving girl. Nancy and Lovey had exclaimed in horror, and even her father had muttered in protest as he'd poked up the fire, though he seldom interfered with what Jennet did. Jennet sometimes thought he was easier on her because of the night her mother died, and she loved him for it. Molly, however, declared that if she must spare Jennet's help, the girl must bring home a halfpenny a day. It was a fair wage for an untrained servant—Jan himself earned only a few pennies a day in the tin mine—but Jennet carried the message to An Marget in shame. However, the woman agreed without comment, and Jennet wondered again why An Marget had accepted her so easily. What was this woman?

In the next few days Jennet saw her as a housewife—quick to spy out dirt, diligent at her spinning wheel; as a gardener—wise in the ways of growing plants and humble enough to muddy her hands in their soil; and as a master of the art of simples—collecting herbs and preparing them for medicines.

Near the end of the second day Jennet saw An Marget as a Charmer. It was a cold, wet day, and Jennet and Marget were working indoors. With the shutters closed against the rain, the candles lit, and the fire leaping in the hearth, the cottage was a cozy place. Marget sat at her spinning wheel, saying little except to murmur to the large brown rabbit which sat watching her. From time to time she fed the rabbit a chunk of something from her pocket. Jennet had noticed that the rabbits never seemed to nibble on the plants in the garden. The cat dozed before the fire, and the magpie was away, to Jennet's relief.

Jennet was working at the black-oak cupboard. Lining its shelves were jars, and it was Jennet's task to memorize the looks of the dried herbs in them. A drawing of the growing plant was pasted on each earthen pot. Humming softly to herself, Jennet worked along the rows, unstopping the jars in turn to pour a few bits into her hand to look at them, feel them, smell them. These yellow-brown crumbles of leaf were rue. These bits of straw were vervain, still lemony-smelling; these red wisps were saffron. Mugwort was powdery with little brown chunks in it. Ragwort was whitish chunks with brown, feathery bits in it. To think these crumbles could cure an ailing body!

Then in the sound of the rain there was a small wailing, and someone beat on the door. An Marget went to open it. Outside stood a little girl, her head shawl dripping with rainwater. She was crying and holding a hand over the other wrist.

"Now, what is it?" An Marget said in a softer voice than Jennet had heard her use.

At the sound, the little girl stumbled forward and buried her head in the old woman's apron.

"It hurts!" she wailed.

An Marget sat in her high-backed chair and took the sobbing child onto her lap. She whispered to her a moment, then examined the wrist. Jennet stepped nearer to watch and caught her breath at the sight of the burned patch—it was so big and red.

Then it happened again. Jennet's own wrist began to tingle and turn red. It began to throb. She almost cried at the fiery pain throbbing in her arm. It was the demon's work, cracking her mind open to other people's pain. Jennet moaned, more in horror at his presence than at the pain.

An Marget didn't notice, all her attention on the little girl in her lap. She laid her hand over the burned place, and the child flinched, but the white witch whispered, "No, now listen well." Softly Marget chanted a charm.

> Three angels came from the north, east, and west.
> One brought fire, another brought ice,
> And the third brought the Holy Ghost.
> So out fire and in frost,
> In the name of the Father, the Son,
>   and the Holy Ghost. Amen.

The woman's rich voice swung with the chant, and the little girl's head nodded with the beat as she stared up at Marget's face. Jennet held her breath. When the voice stopped, the only sound in the room was the purr of the fire in the hearth. Slowly Marget lifted her hand from the child's wrist. The redness of the burn was almost gone. Jennet's eyes widened at the miracle. At the same time, she realized that the pain in her own wrist was gone. The skin was its usual milky-tan.

An Marget stood the little girl on the floor and went to the herb cupboard. Taking out a jar, she smoothed salve over the burned place. The girl didn't wince but wiped her eyes with her other hand and smiled.

"There," Marget whispered.

"Thank you, An Marget!" The little girl hugged the old woman's skirted legs, then stepped back shyly, bobbed a curtsy, and ran out the door.

Jennet stood back by the fire. She looked at the white witch thoughtfully, rubbing a thumb against her chin.

An Marget began to smile. "Yes, Jennet?"

"Well," she said, ". . . the salve. Why? If the salve was needed, why did you speak the charm?"

"Aha!" Marget smacked her hands together. "Good! There's sense in the girl. Yet I will tell you, Jennet, both heal. Do you pray to God?"

Jennet nodded.

An Marget lifted her shoulders. "Well?"

Well . . . Jennet puzzled over the wisewoman's answer. Then as Marget turned back to her spinning wheel Jennet begged, "Mistress Marget, teach me a charm against demons! A demon uses me!"

She told what had happened, showing her wrist, saying, "An evil spirit makes me feel others' pain!"

At first, the woman looked at her in surprise. Then Marget's eyes narrowed. In silence she examined the wrist, where no redness of burn showed now.

At last she said, "How do you know the spirit is evil?"

"But . . . pain?" Jennet protested.

An Marget stepped back, and her eyes looked honestly at Jennet in the dim candlelight.

"This is a mystery," she said. "You want power over mysteries, Jennet, yet I can't explain mysteries in a few words. There's no quick set of words to charm against evil. If you'll be patient and grow with me, you'll learn."

Jennet listened to the crackle of the fire and let her wrist drop. Strangely, she was reassured. Of course, one charm wouldn't be enough against a wicked spirit. An Marget was far ahead of her in understanding the unknown, and she had promised to lead the way.

3

Jennct went to An Sarah Pender's funeral. She
didn't worry that Robin would think she was seeking
him out, for all of the village folk went to one another's
funerals. Kynance Church was nearly full when she got
there except for the pews in front, left empty for the
Pender clan. She slipped into her usual spot, a back pew
opposite a bench end carved with a mermaid. Jennet
liked the mermaid, with her delicious little tail and the
comb and mirror in her hands. Coming into the church
was like coming into a low-vaulted sea cave. Set deep in
the stone walls were slender arched windows of thick
blue-gray glass that let in sea light to the cave, though
on this wet dark day, no light came in at all, and the
church was gloomy.

People coughed and rustled. She saw Nancy and
Will and Lovey across the way, Lovey all decked out in

a fresh white collar. Jennet had on her everyday dress of dark homespun. Her eyes roved until she realized who she was looking for and she looked down at her hands, her cheeks hot. Of course, Robin wouldn't be in the church yet. He'd follow the coffin in with the rest of the Penders.

Now Peter and Paul tolled in the tower, the only church bells left west of St. Ives since the changes in the church. Pastor Thomas' nasal voice began at the church door: " 'I am the resurrection and the life,' saith the Lord . . ."

There was a hasty shuffling in the nave as everyone stood. Fat little Piggy Thomas led the coffin down the center aisle, followed by the Pender men and women from Penmorvah. Jennet saw Robin walking beside a woman with a heavily fleshed face, the flesh wet with tears. Robin's face was serious but his mouth was firm, and he walked with his shoulders back. A fine, upright man, Jennet thought. There was that little golden curl by his ear—she blushed again because Robin's eyes met hers just then.

Lord, he'd winked at her! Right in the middle of a funeral. *Ha*—the beginning of a giggle startled out of her. She caught back the sound and took a deep breath to control herself. When she looked again, Robin was entering a pew. "May you laugh with God," he'd said. So he'd make her laugh right here in church, would he? What could he have meant? Even in the shadows of the church his eyes had sparked green when he'd winked at her.

The Penders filed into their pews, the coffin was left at the head of the aisle, and the service continued. Jennet looked once at the wooden box which held the dead body of Sarah Pender; then she didn't look at it again.

Instead, she looked for the face in the rood screen. The wooden screen was stretched across the church in front of the steps up to the altar, and its top was carved in a frieze of figures. There were a hunter and his dogs, strange beasts, birds, surprising faces, all entwined in leaves and vines. One time her grandmother had told her the hunter was chasing down the evil in the world, and the screen marked the dividing place between the wicked world and the holy altar.

Yes, there was the pisky. Peeping out of the leaves was the puckish face with the pointed ears. Sometimes he seemed to disappear among the twinings. Other times his face popped out and grinned at her when she was praying. Was he laughing with God or—?

Lord, thou hast been our refuge . . . Pastor Thomas was leading the congregation in the responsive reading of the psalm. He was reading the service in English, and some of the older people stumbled, trying to get their mouths around the Saxon words. The old-timers in the village still complained about the changes that had come in the church before Jennet was born.

Once the service had been said in Latin, and a few people could still say some of the strange words. Hearing them, Jennet had tried to imagine the mysterious chantings, appropriate to an awesome God. Then during the change the prayer book had been translated not into Cornish but into that foreign language, English. Jennet had seen men spit and say, "I will speak no Saxon!" But the English words had come into the cottages anyway.

Jennet mouthed the words. She had no trouble reading the service. When she was a child, she'd been shooed into the church along with the other children by Pastor Thomas one evening each week to learn to read the English prayer book and gabble the catechism. The old women would laugh and say, "Piggy Thomas, our troubles don't matter to he, but he do love to tell at the table in St. Ives that all his children read English."

Pastor Thomas was a poor fret of a man, Jennet thought. He had rich relatives in St. Ives who'd gotten him the church living in Kynance, and when he was away, the villagers laughed that Pastor Piggy Thomas was off in St. Ives, larding it up.

Of course, people kept on going to church despite the changes. Kynance Church was the public gathering place, disputes were settled in the courtyard around the roundheaded Celtic cross that stood below the church, and Jennet had seen miracle plays in the church. Saints' days were the people's holidays, and village life went along in the rhythm of the church year. But the worship was habit and lip service. There was no color or power in the church now, and the people reached back to the old beliefs and saints' tales, farther back to the ancient magics.

Jennet wished she could have known the church before the changes made by the English. Her grandmother said then the services were beautiful. When Jennet was a little motherless girl, Grandma'am would hold her on her lap by the fire and tell about those olden days. Then there had been candles on a stone altar and sweet-smelling smoke rising up to the arched ceiling. The priest and his servers wore bright-colored robes and moved in mysterious silences. Grandma'am said then you could feel the Presence of God. When her voice said those words, prickles stood out on Jennet's arms. Other evenings Grandma'am would talk of the ancient time when men had worshiped at the great standing stones out on the moor. In the firelight her voice would croon, "Men bowed down before the stones because God was there. And God looked out of the stones and saw them, whether they were good." Jennet would see it all, under a low gray sky, and she would tremble.

Now is Christ risen from the dead . . .

As Pastor Thomas read the lesson, Jennet heard the wind rising around the church, sounding even through the thick walls. Inside, there was the restless shuffling of people and the whimpers and wails of the Pender women. False tears come easy, Jennet thought. They hadn't spared any attention to An Sarah when she was alive. Just for a moment Jennet let her eyes rest on Rob's back, so broad, tawny head up, listening to the lesson. *Christ risen* . . . Jennet lifted her eyes to the figure in the window of stained glass above the altar. There was Christ on the Cross, with the sun at his left hand, the moon at his right. Vivid color, awful sun and moon glaring . . . the scene always disturbed Jennet. She looked instead for the friendly pisky in the rood screen, but in the dusk of the church the face had disappeared into the leaves.

Everyone knelt for the last prayers, and then Pastor Thomas led the coffin out to the graveyard for the burial service. Jennet knew when Robin went down the aisle with the Penders, but she didn't look at him. There was no sense to it.

As people moved to leave the church, Jennet knelt again briefly. "Thou God," she prayed, "may Thy saints and angels look after Robin Pender. And may they look after me too." She touched the small lump under her dress that was the holed stone. "Let its magic be strong," she added.

In the narrow church porch she edged through the outpouring of villagers. Outside, the rush of wind muffled the murmur of people, and rain blew in gray drifts over the gravestones. The black-robed pastor and the mourners were huddling under the one tree in the churchyard, a tall black yew, whose branches tossed and dripped on the people below. Jennet saw the fresh slit in the earth nearby and thought of the muddy water filling the bottom of the grave. She wouldn't stay for the burial prayers. Pulling her shawl over her hair, she put her head down and started to dash away in the rain.

But a man's arm in gray homespun stretched in front of her, and her heart gave a sudden throb. Robin!

No. She looked up into the bearded face of an old man. It was Uncle Mathy Curnow who had stopped her.

"Now then, girl, are you the one who's gone to Margaret?"

Jennet stared at him, then nodded. Uncle Mathy looked worried. There was a strong smell of ale about him, and his voice was louder than need be, but then Captain Mathy's outdoor voice always sounded as if he were shouting orders.

"I want to talk to you."

He took her by the arm, out of the rain, back into the church porch, cleared now of people. Uncle Mathy was short in the legs, but he still looked down at Jennet. With a clumsy hand he pushed the shawl away from her face and looked closely at her in the shadows.

"What kind of girl are you? Are you a gossip?" His

voice was lower, but it was gruff, and his bushy brows puckered as he watched her.

Jennet let her face stand his scrutiny. "No sir, Uncle Mathy."

"All right, Jennet," he said in a milder tone. "It's just that An Marget is a fine woman. I want you to be good to her."

"Of course." *She*, a rag-tailed girl, be good to the Charmer of Kynance?

The old man sighed. He started to speak, glanced out at the people clustered around the grave in the rain, and turned back to Jennet. He squared his shoulders and spoke brusquely.

"You'll know it sometime, so I'll warn you, girl. Margaret is a good woman, the best in the world, but she has strange fancies. Sometimes she gets to feeling sad and wisht, and a kind of madness comes over her."

"Madness?"

Impatiently he said, "Oh, aye. But the thing is, you be a good girl to her then. Don't let her harm herself."

"Harm—but—"

"Now don't be a silly girl. Keep your wits about you and be good to her." He looked at her sternly and bobbed his beard once for emphasis, then left her.

Jennet stared after the old man. He hurried through the rain to join the village folk around the grave. Then to her surprise she saw men and women draw away from him with hostile looks. She'd never seen Captain

Mathy Curnow treated that way.

But—madness? Jennet's mind fluttered with the thought as she ran through the rain to An Marget's house.

In the next days Jennet watched An Marget for signs of madness, saw none at all, and decided the talk was only an old man's foolishness. True, Marget was silent and remote most of the time, and the way she'd healed the child's burn showed she held strange powers. But she seemed to unbend and warm with interest at Jennet's schooling in herbs. The day after the funeral a woman came seeking a salve for her husband's skin disease. It happened that just the afternoon before Marget had instructed Jennet in the making of skin salve. Instead of rising from her spinning wheel at the woman's plea, An Marget called to Jennet, "Prepare the proper medicine."

Jennet's cheeks tingled with pleasure. It was a test, and she knew just what to do. In a small pot over the fire she put lard to melt, then added fine-cut bits of elder flowers, betony, and other drying herbs. When the potion had seethed, she strained off the ointment and bottled it in a small earthen jar.

The village woman had been shifting her feet while Jennet worked, while Marget's wheel hummed calmly. And the woman looked askance at the pot when Jennet handed it to her.

"Are you sure she did it right?" she demanded of the white witch.

"Jennet has done every step exactly as I would," An Marget assured the woman. "You may rely on the salve."

Jennet twisted her hands as if she'd done something wrong. It was the first time her mistress had praised her, and she hardly knew what to do with her delight.

When the woman was gone, An Marget seemed disposed to chat. Had Jennet ever learned to read? she asked. Could she read English? Jennet was pleased to tell her Yes, that she'd learned from Pastor Thomas, along with the other village children. Though, of course, the only books she'd ever seen were the few English prayer books in the church.

The old woman smiled. "Then you know something I don't," she said.

She could not read English, she told Jennet. Long ago she'd learned to read in the Cornish language, had even studied books of Latin. Hearing this, Jennet thought again of the tales that Marget came from a great family, for only such a girl would be so educated—but that was long before English came to Cornwall in the prayer-book translations.

"Someday you shall read to me," An Marget said.

Another afternoon Jennet saw An Marget as the most sensible woman on the coast. A certain Tom Trevenna from up on the moor came begging the

Charmer's help. His cattle were starving, he said, yet they would not eat the food in their trough. His wife was sick too. They were bewitched, Tom declared. Only the white witch could help.

An Marget gathered some supplies into a pouch, told Jennet to come along, and they walked with Tom over the hills to his moor farm. Although the rain had let up, there was still a small driving drizzle. Yet under her shawl Jennet was warm with satisfaction. She'd been included in Marget's errand of witchcraft. As they neared the cottage, Tom's wife ran out to meet them.

"Oh, thankee, An Marget!" she cried. "Your charms are working already, for the cows have broken out into the fold and are eating like giants. And I feel nearly well."

Jennet looked at her mistress. She had not been aware that Marget had been saying charms as she walked. The wisewoman didn't reply but studied the cows eating the refuse in the stable yard. Then she asked to see the cowhouse. Tom took them into the stone shed built onto the house wall and showed them the trough still full of uneaten fodder.

An Marget looked at it a moment, then took a knife from the pouch that hung at her waist. Just above the trough she plunged the knife into a smeared place in the clay mortar between the stones and dug out a hole. Immediately green stuff ran out of the wall, and a stench filled the low cowshed. When Tom examined the hole, he found a putrid mess of dead rats in the wall. The poison of the mess had been seeping down the wall into the trough, and that was why the cows would not eat.

Jennet could see the sense of it. Yet the Trevennas persisted in praising An Marget for her white witchcraft. Her charms had let her see what was inside the wall, they were sure.

Jennet expected the old woman to protest and explain. Instead, Marget looked straight at the Trevennas with her strong face and gravely accepted their thanks. No pay was offered to the white witch, but Jennet knew that a thanksgiving would appear on the doorstep at Chelew, yarn for her knitting, or perhaps a sack of grain.

As they walked away from the cottage, An Marget laughed suddenly at Jennet, who was still glancing at her, puzzled.

"You'll wear a hole in my head, staring at me so much, girl. Don't you understand? Faith heals."

And then, as Jennet puckered her brows, the woman added impatiently, "A white witch has power if people believe in her power."

The drizzling rain had stopped, and the sky had lifted to its proper place over the moor, the wind tearing the clouds into gray wisps. Although the sun was still obscured, the late afternoon light increased until the high moorland was strangely potent with color. Greens were brilliant; the gorse glowed intensely yellow and gave off the piercing smell of spiced honey. Jennet sucked in the smell, like a sip of the sweetness. She felt as vividly alive as the moor, as if she could whirl and dance. What a good life it was, learning to be a white witch! At the Trevenna cottage she had been accepted and honored as the assistant to the Charmer of Kynance. And An Marget was the wisest of all women! Jennet opened her mouth and sang out the high clear music of a ballad, her voice dipping and rising like a bird on the breeze.

To Jennet's surprise, Margaret joined in the song, and when Jennet, laughing and singing, looked at her, the woman nodded and sang on with a curious eagerness.

Then when An Marget said, "Down yonder amongst the rocks grows club moss, and I need some," Jennet found an excuse to run. She picked up her skirts and raced down the hill, tossing her hair in the wind. Margaret ran after her, light-footed as any girl.

Jennet laughed as she ran. Now anyone seeing them couranting on the moor would think he'd found two mad witches for sure.

But when they reached the vale where the moss grew in crevices of rock, An Marget calmed her breathing and turned to her work.

"Club moss will heal all diseases of the eye," she instructed Jennet. "But the taking of the moss is not lightly done. I will teach you the mystery."

The moss must be cut at sundown on the third day of the moon, An Marget said. First the old woman washed her hands carefully at the stream that ran down the cleft between the hills. Next she took the knife from her pouch, and after washing it, held it up to the sky, where a thin crescent of moon showed through a veil of clouds. In a loud voice she said:

> *As Christ healed the issue of blood,*
> *Do thou cut what thou cuttest for good!*

Then she knelt and cut off a clump of the moss, which she wrapped in a white cloth. She also drew a small bottle from the pouch and sent Jennet to the stream to fill it, for, she said, the moss must be boiled in water taken nearest to its place of growth.

Jennet had watched, entranced. The woman with the knife lifted to the daytime moon, the mystery . . . Jennet trembled as she knelt at the stream, and the call of a cuckoo drifted on the air. She saw the bird far above on a pile of boulders crowning the tor. She called "Cuc-coo!" and the bird repeated its solitary cry, "Cuc-coo." Then it flew away.

Jennet realized it was the first cuckoo she had heard this spring. Its cry meant that summer was coming. As she stoppered the bottle of water she smiled, remembering the tale of some foolish Kynance men who had tried to wall in a cuckoo to keep summer forever.

Yet the cuckoo was a twofold symbol, and Jennet stopped smiling, thinking about it. The first call of the cuckoo was ominous, too, for it heralded May Day. Before the delights of summer must come Walpurgis Night, eve of the first day of May. On that night, witches were said to ride their sticks and meet in covens in deserted places. Over at Penmorvah there was a whole flock of black witches who might ride out. On the last day of April, Molly and the girls—all of the village women—would gather elder leaves and fasten them to the windows and doors to ward off the evil of witches. That night they would sweep out the house with special bundles of twigs, for a witch might have crept in, concealed in the shape of a mouse or a bug.

It was an evil night, and yet Jennet wondered about it. On that night, too, men and women ventured out into the dark to light May Day fires on the hilltops.

When Jennet rejoined An Marget, she saw the woman was looking toward the crown of rocks set against the sky, where the cuckoo had been. She was humming the ballad again with that strange eagerness.

Jennet watched the woman as she said, "Soon it will be May Day."

"Aye, my feasten-day will come!" Margaret breathed the words, eyes still lifted to the tor.

Then she looked at Jennet, and she frowned. "Ho, I see what you're thinking. Do you really believe I would fly around on a silly broomstick?" she demanded. "Or change myself into a bat?" Her strong nose beaked forward.

Jennet looked down in shame. She couldn't picture the wisewoman doing such undignified things. And yet—

"But they say that witches—" she blundered and stopped.

"Pshaw!"

An Marget didn't speak again on the way home. The light on the moor had faded, and the lightness of her mood was gone. Jennet told herself she'd done nothing to feel in disgrace, but the feeling of closeness with the white witch was lost. Yet, upon reaching the village, An Marget told Jennet to come along with her to see how the moss should be brewed.

Inside the cottage, she set Jennet to lighting candles against the dark, while she stirred up the fire. The candlelight brought gleams from the brass on the shelf, but it deepened the shadows, and the flames from the fireplace made them move.

"Welcome," said a low voice.

Jennet dropped the lighting-taper. Then she discovered the magpie in the shadows, sitting on top of the oak cupboard. Malachai's eyes were bright yellow in the firelight. On the floor below the bird sat the gray cat, as if the two were in league. She saw other movements in the shadows, the stirrings of rabbits, the whiteness of a lamb, a flutter overhead which she hoped was only a robin. An Marget's creatures were gathered, waiting for her.

The woman motioned Jennet to the hearth. Jennet brought the bottle of spring water, and An Marget poured it into the black kettle hanging over the fire. When she added the club moss, she murmured words so rapidly that Jennet couldn't understand them. She wondered if the words were a necessary charm, but she was afraid to ask, for the old woman's manner had become agitated. Her hands shook, and she stirred the brew with impatient thrusts. Then she sprang up from the hearth and paced the length of the room twice, twisting her hands and moving her head in some kind of distress. Abruptly she halted before the oak dresser and looked up at the magpie.

Her voice came out hard, gutteral. "Will he come?"

Malachai looked down at her, yellow eyes unwinking. "He will come," the bird spoke.

The woman gasped. She cried, "Will you come?"

"Aye, Margaret, I will come." The voice was distant.

At that, the woman uttered a long wail as she stood motionless. Then she ran out the door, into the night.

Jennet had backed against the hearth wall. The wail seemed still to quiver in the shadows. She stared up at the black bird, her eyes opening wider and wider. The magpie cocked its head and looked down at her with one eye that flickered. It was a demon. She couldn't stay here with a demon. The gray cat slipped out the door after her mistress, and the other beasts made worried stirrings and sounds. Jennet ran out the door, and even the dense darkness outside was a relief from the unrest of the room behind.

Then she heard pebbles scattering on the path that led from the cottage to the cliff above. An Marget was running up the path to the cliffs over the sea, alone, in darkness. Jennet remembered Uncle Mathy's warning: "Madness. Don't let her harm herself."

But—to follow a madwoman! Jennet began to shiver, and she clasped her arms across her chest to stop the trembling. An Marget was so good, so wise. And now—solid rock had turned suddenly to a bog.

A lamenting cry drifted down to her. An Marget was running, wailing, on the cliff's edge. She might throw herself into the sea.

"G-Go after her." Her teeth chattered.

The woman had talked to a spirit. Through Malachai she had communed with a spirit, and the spirit had promised to come. Who? What kind of thing from the darkness? An Marget was crying in terrible distress. She didn't have power over darkness, after all.

Jennet fled to her father's house.

4

She was a traitor. The next morning the thought was so disgusting Jennet couldn't bear it in her mind. She imagined that she'd acted otherwise. Of course she wouldn't run away, forsaking a friend . . . well, not a friend, she couldn't claim that, but . . . No, she'd stayed, she'd been faithful. She'd watched on the cliff in the dark with An Marget, and she'd led her mistress safely back to the cottage . . . If only she had.

Jennet ran along the path to Chelew. Had Marget fallen into the sea? Been carried away by the spirit? It was a clear day after the rain, soft blue sky above, sensible daylight shining on the cows in the pastures. Such terrible things couldn't have happened. She'd been a fool. An Marget had just been upset about something. Jennet slowed to step over a stone stile between the fields and pulled a gorse blossom from the hedge. She sucked the sweet flower. The sweetness was real. A wisewoman finding dead rats in a wall, that was real.

"Lord God, help her," Jennet whispered. God was real.

And there weren't such things as demons?

Jennet came around to the corner under the cliff where Chelew was tucked. There was no smoke from the chimney of the cottage. The window shutters were still closed and so was the door. No chickens scratched in the dooryard. The wind wuthered faintly beyond the rise of cliff. Jennet stood still and looked at the place, seemingly deserted. What had happened here after she'd run away? Cautiously she approached the door and knocked.

There was only the sound of the distant wind; then a voice from within said, "Who's there?" and Jennet's heart jumped with relief.

"It's me, Jennet."

There was another silence. Jennet couldn't hear any sounds of movement inside.

Then An Marget said, "Go away." There was no inflection to her voice.

Jennet stared at the rough wooden door. "Forever?" she cried.

"Come back after May Day."

Jennet listened for more words, but none came. "An Marget," she called, "I'm sorry I ran away." She waited. There was only silence within.

At last, she turned and walked slowly back toward the village. She didn't know what to make of it all. Perhaps An Marget was punishing her. Fair enough. But why after May Day? Her feasten-day, she'd said. And the evil night that came before it, that was tomorrow night. Jennet found herself imagining all kinds of things and made herself stop. She could imagine anything, but she knew nothing.

It was a fresh day for roaming the cliffs. Jennet considered taking the holiday, but somehow she had no heart for being alone. Instead, she went home for a bite to eat. She'd missed supper last night, and she'd been in too much of a hurry this morning for breakfast.

However, as she spooned porridge from the pot, she wondered if it was worth it. Lovey was idling around the room, exclaiming "At the funeral, Robin—" and "Robin told me—" and then Molly set in to nag Jennet about An Marget.

"Just as well she doesn't need you today. The pennies aren't worth it," Molly declared. She smoothed her tousled hair righteously. "You'll get yourself in trouble, Jen, mixing up with that old witchwoman. They say she's up to wickedness."

Jennet's lips tightened. She set the bowl on the rough table and began to eat. Lovey pulled up a stool opposite her.

"What wickedness, hey, Jennie?" Lovey propped her elbows on the table, chin in hands. "Tell us about it! What about that bottle old Maggie gave Uncle Mathy?"

"Yes, what about it?" Moll came to stand over her.

Jennet flung herself up from their crowding. "Nothing! She's a good woman, and you'd say so, too, the minute you wanted her help."

She started out the doorway, but Molly called her back.

"Here, Mistress Smart, if you're going out, make use of yourself. Take this grain up to the mill."

Well, it was something to do. Jennet took the sack and looked around for Jemmy and Dick. She wouldn't mind their company. But they'd gone off somewhere to play.

It was a short walk up the stream bank to the mill. Here in the fold of hills where the valley narrowed, the growth was more lush, almost gloomy with elder and beech trees around the millpond. Though today the sun made the new leaves glisten, and in the dappled shade under the trees, yellow and pink wild flowers grew in thickets of ivy and pond grasses. Here children hunted in the spring for the first flowers and searched in summer, usually in vain, for strawberries. Here in the evenings courting lads and girls idled around the pond.

But in the daytime the mill was a busy place. Over the swish of the wheel Jennet heard the high chatter of woman-talk. Sitting on a low wall near the stone mill-house was the usual cluster of women and girls waiting for their grain to be ground. The tavern was the men's gossiping place, and the mill was the women's.

Today's gossip must be especially good, for the women were clacking away and waving their arms. Jennet recognized the two worst gossips in the village, Gracey Winkey, who was always blinking her eyes, and Dolly the Duck. With so many surnames the same in Kynance, nicknames were handy. As Jennet walked closer, the chatter stopped short, leaving Gracey Winkey's squeal hanging in midair:

"There's the witch-girl now!"

One little girl tittered in the sudden hush, but another child drew back from Jennet fearfully.

After the nerve-wrack of last night and this morning, Jennet had rather looked forward to the everyday talk at the mill. She glanced around for someone to sit with, perhaps Anne Pendower, the tavern-keeper's daughter. Anne was a quiet girl, and sometimes they exchanged fancies. But Jennet couldn't see a friendly face. Everyone was watching her as if she might turn into a toad at any moment.

"Is that old Mag's grain?" Gracey Winkey said, thrusting out a skinny arm and blinking rapidly. "Good thing you're last. It might foul the millstone!" She cackled and nodded, looking around at the others for approval.

They murmured, and one woman declared, "I'll never go to that black witch again."

"I can brew simples as well as she," Dolly said in her quacking voice.

Jennet was confused by the attack. She retreated a little and sat down on a stone by the edge of the water, as if by choice. An Marget had always been respected, even revered. Not come to the white witch? Black witch? Jennet realized that since she'd started to work for An Marget, only three persons had sought the woman's services, the little girl, the woman for the skin salve, and Tom Trevenna from the isolated moor cottage.

A loud groan came from Gracey Winkey. "Ohh, there's that pain again!" She rubbed her neck. "It's Mag's doing, I say! Her and Mathy and that bottle of magic water."

"Aye! She's bewitched us!"

Other women winced and cried out, rubbing their necks and shoulders.

"Who hasn't cursed Mathy's pesky cows? Could we help it if the curse was spoken in the evil moment?"

"Aye, anyone could be the ill-wisher. But that don't mean we'd overlook Mathy's cows with witchcraft."

Jennet saw that it was for her benefit; yet the women really did seem to twitch with pains.

Gracey Winkey blinked at Jennet and raised her fist. "Tell Marget to uncork that bottle, girl. If she don't, I'll get my husband, and he'll burn her house down!"

"Oliver—that old timnoodle," said Dolly the Duck, with the comfortable scorn of a widow woman.

"Yes, he will, Doll! I'll see to it!" Gracey said. "Go tell her now, you Jennet Trevail!"

Jennet sprang up. "Go tell her yourself! You know she's a good woman."

She wouldn't stay out here and listen to all this hatefulness. She ran into the mill. Maybe Jack would take her out of turn.

"Please," she begged the miller.

He was a young married man. "I will for a kiss from that pretty face," he said, grinning. Then he looked at her again in the shadows of the mill and seemed to remember who she was. "Never mind," he said hastily, taking her sack.

Jennet put her cold hands to her burning cheeks. He didn't want a kiss from a witch-girl. Lord, she wouldn't kiss that silly fool anyway!

Through the doorway she could see the women had their heads together, muttering and nodding in excitement. Jennet stepped to the side of the door, out of sight, and listened to the clack.

"Get your men to go up to the stream-works and make Captain Mathy uncork the bottle," Dolly urged. "That's the idea."

The women chattered. "Aye, my Bob would do it, he's that angry!"

"No," Gracey Winkey said. "Mathy Curnow's got

a strong moor house up there on Bostrella Downs and a good crew of men. They'd fight. I know a better way."

Her voice dropped, and Jennet strained to hear.

Even Gracey's whisper was piercing. ". . . the bottle . . . break the spell . . . throw fire over the witch . . ."

"Aye, aye, that's right!"

"Or stick a pin in Mag to the bone, draw blood." Dolly chuckled. "That'll break a witch's spell, right enough."

Jennet's mouth crinkled in disgust. But her lips stayed parted as she listened, for it was more than talk. They were making a plan; the women were agreeing. When their men came in from the fields and the fishing boats this evening, they'd march on Chelew. They'd throw fire over the witch to break the spell of the bottle that was tormenting them all.

"Here 'tis. Took my share."

Jennet started as the miller spoke from behind her and thrust out the sack of flour. He looked at her dubiously, as if she might put the evil eye on him.

"Many thanks," Jennet said wryly. Probably he'd taken more than his share, to pay for his doubts.

The talk outside stopped as she ran out of the mill and down the path. In silence, the women watched her go by. When she had passed, she turned back to them. You'd better not! she wanted to shout, but what could she say that would have any effect? Some of the women were pulling their shawls over their faces, to ward off her stare. Jennet whirled and ran on down the stream bank to her house.

She dropped the sack inside the door and hurried away, to avoid conversation. On the path she dithered, trying to decide which way to go. Should she run to Chelew to warn An Marget? She thought of the closed house and the mystery there. Farfetched ideas flickered: She saw herself running to Robin Pender for help, saw herself kneeling in the church to pray, appealing to Pastor Thomas. Uncle Mathy—that was it. ". . . good crew . . . they'd fight," Gracey had said. Yes, Captain Mathy Curnow would protect his old friend Margaret.

Hurrying, Jennet took the path that led up through the hills behind Kynance Churchtown. On a weekday he was sure to be at the tinworks on Bostrella Downs. It was a rocky, barren hill she climbed, with a ground cover of short, tough furze bushes and fronds of bracken. The path was barely visible as it twisted through the brambles, but Jennet knew her way well enough. She came out on the bare top, and the wind was a steady pressure at her back as she ran over the moor that spread away to the southeast. Ahead, silhouetted against the sky, was a circle of standing stones. They were lean boulders of gray granite, taller than she, spaced like a circle of giant men holding council. The Old Men had set them up, people said. Jennet liked to think they were the doing of Boclas. Perhaps the stones were the base of a great watchtower the old giant had erected. From the tower, Boclas had looked out over all the countryside and the sea, watching for invaders, so as to protect the people of Kynance.

Boclas—had the Spirit at the Logan Rock been only a gull? Yet she'd seen the Rock move. Now Jennet didn't know whether the giant had rejected her or not.

When Jennet reached the circle, she left the path, walked between two hulking stones, and stood in the center of the circle. Some of the boulders seemed like rough-hewn faces watching her. Here the wind whispered off the stones.

"Boclas, protect us now," she pleaded.

Then she ran on toward Bostrella Downs. She thought of An Marget, silent in her silent house. And in the village this sudden hatred—sparking, crackling— men and women gathering to march on their good Charmer. If only she hadn't given Mathy the bottle. . . . But Uncle Mathy would stop them. *I'll save you, An Marget!* Jennet leaped over some rocks in excitement. She was no traitor.

The way led over a hill and then up a stream to the tinworks. The stream bed below was cluttered with rubble from the mining. Above, she saw the men working in their high boots, shoveling at the tin earth.

Good! They weren't all drunk in the moor house, then, but their wits sharp with the open air. This tin streaming was no underground mine such as her father worked in. Here the men had simply dug shallow trenches in the ground and were tossing shovelfuls of earth onto the tye, an inclined plane of boards over which ran water diverted from the stream. Uncle Mathy was working at the tye, turning the earth over and over with his shovel, so that the cascade of water would wash away the lighter waste and leave behind the tin.

Jennet looked at the bearded man with relief as he stood stocky as a rock, roaring an order to a man in the trench. Up here he was *Captain* Mathy, not just an old uncle of the village.

"Matthew Curnow!" she called as she ran stumbling over the stream-bed trash.

"Ho!" he shouted, spying her. "What's the matter?"

"An Marget! She ——"

"Shut back the water, Jack!" Mathy turned his ruddy face to Jennet and gave her his attention.

"It's your bottle. At the mill . . ." Jennet told what she'd heard the women planning, while the three men of the crew came to listen.

Captain Mathy sighed out a long whistle. "Say, boys, want a fight?"

"Hurrah!" The men threw down their picks and shovels and stopped only long enough to run to the moor house for a jug of ale.

"Hurt Marget!" Mathy bellowed as he tramped across the moor. "Stick her with a pin, you say? Burn her out! They forgot about Mathy Curnow! Hurry up there, you Jack Tregear. Never mind that jug."

Jennet had to run to keep up with the men. Near Kynance, they circled the village, not to give away Marget had help, Captain Mathy said. When they reached Chelew, the shutters of the cottage were still closed, and none of Marget's animals were in sight. A stray finger of wind had slipped around the cliff and tapped a vine against the wooden shutter of one window, the only sound in the silence. It was midafternoon by now, and the sky had changed from soft blue to a hazy yellow. A glimpse of the sea around the cliff showed a low bank of clouds rising on the horizon.

While Jack Tregear and the other men stood back, Captain Mathy knocked on the door. Jennet waited for a sound from within. Now Mathy might find out that she'd run away last night, despite his warning that she must take care of Margaret when she was feeling wisht. Jennet glanced at the burly man out of the corners of her eyes. She wouldn't put it past Uncle Mathy to whip her if Margaret had come to harm.

"Hey now, Marget, where are you?" he shouted. "It's your old friend, Mathy Curnow, out here."

The door opened. An Marget stood in the dusk of the closed cottage, where there was no firelight, no candlelight. Her face was calm, and she looked at Mathy and Jennet without expression. Then a private smile tipped her lips, but it didn't reach her eyes.

"Well, Matthew, come to join the fun?"

He had started to blurt out the news but stopped. "What's this? You know?"

She stepped back into the grayness of the cottage and beckoned Mathy and Jennet to follow. On a table, Jennet saw the hourglass which usually sat on the fireplace mantle. The woman turned the glass, and the sand began its downward sifting.

"Before those sands are down," An Marget said, "you will share the evil events the stars have marked for me."

Jennet stared at the wisewoman. No mad disarray showed in her face or clothing. An Marget was as calm and neat as ever, glossy hair showing at her forehead under her hood. Yet there was a distant coldness about her. How had she known? Jennet wondered if some loving child from the village had run and told her. Or had she learned by white witchcraft? *White* arts, Jennet told herself severely. She'd just noticed markings in the ashes on the hearth, as if figures had been drawn in the gray ash with a stick.

Captain Mathy was filling the chilly cottage with his blustering worry for Margaret. Gracey Winkey and all her crew were coming to throw fire on the witch, he declared, full of indignation. Did she know that?

Yes, she did.

"Bad business," he added uneasily. "Shall I uncork the bottle, hey, Marget?"

She looked at him from the shadow of her hood and smiled faintly again. "Are your cattle well, then, fat and thriving? Has the ill-wisher removed his spell?"

The old man was pricked. "No, by God!" he roared. "Those cows are puny as ever! Marget, we can fight that crew. It's just that I don't want them down on you, old girl."

"Nay, you'll not fight." The woman lifted her head. "I will. It's time those village fools remembered my power."

Jennet chilled, watching An Marget. The woman took no notice of her, as if she were a stranger.

She told Captain Mathy to have his men wait behind the cottage, out of sight, and Jennet saw him obey, sheepish as a boy. Politely, Margaret said that Matthew and Jennet might wait in the cottage with her, but she lit no candles. Leaving the door open, Margaret seated herself in the tall oak chair. She sat erect, eyes on the falling sand in the hourglass. Jennet found a stool and sat down to wait, but Uncle Mathy stumped up and down the room.

"Now, Marget, we must plan how to handle this."

She turned her eyes to him. "Matthew Curnow, sit

down on the settle and be quiet." She spoke smoothly, but there was that hard base to her voice. "I appreciate your good heart, but it is I who will handle this."

Mathy sat; he and Jennet waited with the Charmer of Kynance. Outside, the light faded, and the room grew darker. A rabbit crouching by the cold hearth didn't stir. The room was so quiet Jennet could hear the whisper of the flowing sand. Glancing about, Jennet saw Malachai perched on top of the cupboard. It shocked her that the magpie could have been there all the time, so still she hadn't known of its presence. The bird's clear eye watched her, and she looked away. She didn't want to remember Malachai's voice last night and the way An Marget had reacted.

Jennet looked at the old woman. Not old, ageless. She sat in the high-backed armchair like a queen, remote as a queen. No movement of emotion showed on her strong face, not even a shadow flickered by the carved nose. An Marget watched the sand as if the grains fell by her will. Jennet wondered what she was thinking. From what source was she drawing strength? Her power, she'd said. The villagers must remember her power. And where did she get her power?

Jennet sprang up and walked in agitation to the end of the room, back again. An Marget glanced at her but said nothing. Deliberately Jennet stooped by the hearth and let her skirt sweep away the drawings in the cold ashes. Marget took no notice.

She *is* a good woman, Jennet thought. I must be sensible, as An Marget is sensible. Always Marget had used her powers for good, to help people.

Impulsively Jennet asked, "May I have a drink of water?"

To her gratification, An Marget got up and brought her a cupful from the bucket. The woman didn't speak or smile, but she did the service, and Jennet felt eased.

Uncle Mathy welcomed the break in the tension. "Marget, I—" he began. Then voices sounded outside.

"Mathy!" Jack Tregear called in warning from behind the house.

"Come out of there, you old witch!" came Gracey Winkey's shrill voice.

Jennet started angrily. How dared she talk to the Charmer that way! She ran to the doorway, and Captain Mathy jostled past her.

Marching down the path was a rabble of village folk. Gracey Winkey led them, stepping along like a crow, switching her black skirts. Behind her came men carrying burning sticks. One of them was Gracey's little bandy-legged husband, Oliver. There were women, too, squealing and shaking their fists while the men rumbled threats. Last of all, around the path came Dolly the Duck. At the sight of the waddling woman, Jennet giggled suddenly, hysterically.

"Look at the devil-girl laugh!" Gracey shrieked, blinking furiously at Jennet. "Throw fire on her too!"

"First the witch! Break her spell!"

"Fire the thatch!"

In a fury of excitement the shouting men and women milled in the dooryard, which had seemed so deserted earlier. Their burning sticks waved and smoked over their heads. A hen flew squawking from under a bush, and a rabbit leapt away.

"There goes the witch in disguise! Get her!"

Captain Mathy stood, feet apart, on the flat stone before the door and shouted, "Jack! After them, boys!"

"Mathy, stop."

An Marget stepped through the doorway, unhurried, motioning the old man aside. Quietly she took his place on her doorstone and watched the crowd. An intensity of filtered late-afternoon light made the twisted faces peculiarly vivid.

At the sight of Marget the people drew back for a moment, hushed; then they surged forward.

"The witch!"

"Uncork that bottle!"

"Remove your spell, or we'll throw fire on you!"

"Prick her, Gracey!" called Dolly. "Here's the pin."

Malachai flew through the doorway and perched on the roof over An Marget's head.

"Wicked! Wicked!" cried the bird.

Shouts fell to murmurs, as the folk stared.

"Lord God!" Oliver exclaimed, crossing himself and nearly dropping his flaming torch.

"Her familiar!" Gracey screamed. She snatched up a stone and flung it at the magpie, who screeched in return.

Bouncing harmlessly on the thatched roof, the stone fell at An Marget's feet. Jennet and Mathy jumped protectively toward Marget, but she lifted her head and held them off with a look. Moving deliberately, she picked up the stone and looked at the village people until men began to move uneasily and women's squeals dropped. She cupped the rock in her hand and held it up to them.

"Is this your offering for my doorstep?" She tossed it on the ground. Jennet saw the woman smile secretly, lids drooping to veil her eyes. "You fools."

"Stick her—" Dolly's squawk died as Marget shot a look at her. Hastily the fat woman pulled her shawl over her face to ward off the look.

Light flared suddenly on Chelew as the sun sank below the cloud bank and seemed to rest on the ocean. A golden stream pointed level across the water to the scene in the dooryard. In the flood of light An Marget extended her arm and pointed at Gracey Winkey.

Her voice deep and measured, she said, "Now comes the hour of sweet rest for man and beast. And now comes the power to blast and ban."

She took a step forward, and Gracey Winkey shrank back from the pointing finger. Marget spoke louder. "My curse descend upon the arm that cast that stone!

Before three moons have come and gone, thine arm, from fingertips to shoulder blade, shall wither and waste to skin and bone."

The magpie flapped and shrieked on the roof, as if to add to the witch's curse.

The people gasped, faces twisted now with fear. Even Uncle Mathy stared at An Marget as she stood with set face, arm still lifted.

"Oliver," Gracey Winkey whimpered. "Stop her."

Her husband dropped his torch, shaking his head. "Come away, foolish woman! Come away!" His skinny legs scampered to the path.

Holding her arm close to her side, Gracey looked at An Marget, blinking. Then she whirled her skirts and ran after Oliver. The others followed in a rout, running and screaming.

"Ha ha ha!" Hands on hips, An Marget roared with laughter like a man. "Look at them run! The sheep!"

Jennet had never seen the woman laugh so heartily. Yet this wasn't the warmth of Robin's laughter. Jennet put her fingers to her lips, slid her teeth on a fingernail as she watched Marget. The brilliant light calmed as the red sun sank below the ocean rim.

Uncle Mathy stirred at last. "Marget, that wasn't wise—" he began.

"You can take your boys home now," An Marget said, laughing easily. "They'll have to find their own fights."

He hesitated, frowned, then went to speak to his men, who had watched from the corner of the house. Malachai chattered something at him as he went past. Jennet looked apprehensively at the magpie, then at the woman. There was something she had to ask, and she feared to.

"An Marget—" she started.

Marget held up her hand. "Wait."

She watched the pathway to the village. In a moment a man came around the curve of the hill, and Marget nodded. It was Oliver, "that old timnoodle," who came creeping along the path. At the sight of the white witch he tried to turn back, but Gracey Winkey's face appeared at the curve, hissing at him, urging him on. Other of the women leaned around behind her to watch. Miserably, the little man approached the woman on her doorstone. At the edge of the dooryard he stopped and spoke, looking at the ground.

"If it please, Mistress Marget, take the curse off of Gracey." He looked up at her, pleading. "She's sorry, for sure. She'll never say a word against you again."

An Marget chuckled. "And why is Gracey Winkey suddenly so sorry?"

His eyes flicked at her fearfully and away. "It's the pain!" he exclaimed. "Already her arm hurts so bad she can't lift it. And she can't open her fingers. Lift the curse, An Marget! We'll give you anything you ask!"

Jennet drew in her breath. Already! She stepped

back from the woman. Now she knew why An Marget had given the bottle to Uncle Mathy. Marget had known all this would result.

An Marget looked at the frightened man steadily. "I'll have none of your gifts. But I will lift the curse if you'll promise me this: Not you, not Gracey," her voice grew louder, "not one of that rabble who came here shall ever ill-wish anyone again."

"No, no!" he muttered. "We didn't, we won't! Never!"

"No." She laughed. "You won't dare."

Then she gave him instructions. Gracey Winkey should stroke her arm with the first buttercup she found, and the pain would be gone by the time she reached home. Oliver nodded, bobbing thank-you's, and ran back to the group on the path, hurrying them away.

Uncle Mathy and his men took their leave of Marget. As they, too, went up the path, An Marget called after them.

"You can uncork that bottle now, Mathy."

He turned and looked at her, then nodded. "Aye, Marget."

Jennet was left alone with her mistress. Now it was even harder to ask the question. She touched the holed stone for courage and found she'd lost faith in the stone. Marget had turned to her, watching her, for the first time today all her attention concentrated on

Jennet. Jennet took short breaths. Holding her head up, she said it rapidly.

"An Marget, where do you get your power? Who is your master?"

The cliffs were pink and softened in the evening light, and the sound of the wind had hushed away. In the quiet a bird murmured as it drifted toward its nest. An Marget looked intently at Jennet, the light flecking in her hazel eyes. Jennet looked away from the eyes. She stared at the curve of the hawk nose. There was a deep line by Marget's mouth. The mouth moved.

"I'll tell you, Jennet Trevail. No one. Not the Devil. No one is my master."

Jennet looked back at the flecked eyes, and a breath sighed out of her. Not the Devil! She stared at the woman. No one?

An Marget's face relaxed, and she smiled in gentle awareness of the girl. "Go home in safety, Jennet. You don't need to fear the darkness with me."

Unconsciously Jennet humped and stretched her shoulders as the tension went out of them. The sun was down. Now it was the Sabbath.

"All right, An Marget!"

5

It was Sunday morning, and Pastor Thomas was scolding his flock from the pulpit.

"Now I don't want to hear a word about my people building May Day fires tonight and doing wicked, pagan things." He sniffed uneasily. "There's no such thing as Walpurgis Night."

Unfortunately he sneezed, and someone in the pews tittered.

Jennet smiled. No, Piggy Thomas, you won't hear a word about it, she thought, and you won't see a thing if you stay fast in your house.

She sat in a back pew with her family. Turning her head, she could see Robin sitting in the mermaid pew. Such a tawny head. She couldn't see his eyes, but what a firm profile he had. Then she noticed that Lovey, next to her, had her head turned too, looking at him.

Flushing, Jennet jerked her head to the front. Now wasn't that a pretty sight for the folk in church to see! Both unwed Trevail girls gawking at rich Robin Pender.

After church no one wanted to go home—the air was so soft and there was so much to talk about. Men and women in their Sunday homespun stood in clusters in the churchyard, whispering about Gracey Winkey and the white witch, and they glanced at Jennet as she passed. She hesitated, waiting for her family, then decided to go home without the others. Nancy was standing with Will, lifting her face like the first-blooming rose, and Jan, Moll, and Lovey were visiting with friends. However, Jemmy and Dick were skittering about the graveyard, chasing each other around the headstones, sliding on the slabs of slate that lay flat over the graves, and Molly told Jennet to catch them.

She snatched Jemmy off a roundheaded cross and held tight to his tugging hand while she tried to coax Dick down from the lowest branch of the yew tree. As she stood there she became aware that people nearby were talking about something besides the events of last night. Robin Pender's name caught her attention.

"He can't find the money," a woman was saying. "Someone's stolen it."

"Maybe there wasn't any money, after all," a man said.

Dolly the Duck was part of the group. "Now you

know An Sarah Pender had money," she declared. "She had a whole bagful of coin hidden away. Besides, Robin Pender gave her his savings for safekeeping, and he can't find that either."

"Like I said, somebody's stolen it."

"Maybe An Marget spirited it away," Dolly said, smacking her lips. Then she saw Jennet and added hastily, "No, Marget wouldn't do that, not she."

Pastor Thomas came hurrying through the church-yard, pompous and round and black. Whichever group of folk he bounced up to, the buzzing stopped. Of course, no one had told him a word about last night's doings at Chelew. Jennet saw Gracey Winkey smooth her arm and turn away as the little pastor came in her direction. He veered past Jennet and saw her tending her brothers.

"Good girl, good girl," he said vaguely, nodding.

She doubted he was even aware that she was work-ing for An Marget, though she supposed the pastor knew something of the white witch's reputation. After all, he and Marget had both lived here for years. But she'd never heard of him preaching against the Charmer.

Jennet saw her father looking at her across the gravestones. He must be ready to leave. She didn't have his attention often—Jan Trevail worked too hard to be much of a family man—and she hurried the little boys along to join him and Molly. However, he continued to look at her without smiling. Uneasily, she turned to hand the boys over to Molly, and Jemmy tugged at his mother's hand like a ball bouncing on a string, repeating, "I'm hungry! Let's go!"

Lovey was staring at her too. Then her eyes flitted away, and her round face dimpled. "Rob-Bob!" she said. "Will you dance with me at Nancy's wedding?"

Robin came strolling up, grinning. He always looked so alive, Jennet thought, and most so when he was smiling—the lean lines of his face, the way his mouth curled and his eyes sparkled at you—there was a teasing awareness to his smile.

He was smiling at Lovey. "Yes, Mistress Loveday, I'll dance with you."

There was something thick in Jennet's throat. She turned away and felt fingers on her arm.

"I'll dance with any pretty girl who asks me." Robin's eyes narrowed as he looked down at her, and the green light in them flickered at her.

"I—I don't—I couldn't—" she stammered.

"Come home, Jennet," Jan Trevail said heavily.

Jennet found out the trouble on the way home. As soon as the Trevails were away from the church square and walking up the path along the stream, Molly started in on Jennet.

"Fine doings at Chelew last night!" she exclaimed. "And you in the middle of it all!"

"You're a disgrace to the family," Lovey said primly.

"Jennet's bad. I'm hungry," Jemmy declared.

Jan's voice thudded through the chatter like a blunt axe. "I won't have it."

That should have been enough. Jennet felt as if a weight had crushed her to the ground. But Molly had a lot more to say.

Her voice rose. "That An Marget means trouble. You'll do yourself no good with her. Or with those men of Uncle Mathy's. Couranting around on the downs with those drunken stream-workers! I heard about that, too, mind you!"

"Everybody's talking about how you're a witch-girl," Lovey said.

Everybody? What did Robin think?

"An Marget's a powerful woman, but we don't know what she's up to," Molly shrilled. "You, Jennet, you stay away from her. You're not to work for her any more."

They'd reached the house. Jan said, "You'll stay home."

He shoved her through the doorway with such force that she stumbled across the room and fell against the table. He'd never been rough with her. From the dirt floor she looked up at his eyes in the lined face.

"Father?" she cried.

He turned away. Jennet got up and climbed the ladder to the talfat, wincing because her shoulder hurt where it had struck the table. From the rough flooring above, she stared down at her father. Jan didn't give a look her way, but sat down at the table to wait for his food. He said nothing more, ignoring the chatter of the women and children around him.

Jennet took off her Sunday dress and put on her everyday clothes. She waited in the dimness above while Jan ate and then left to go down to the tavern. When he had gone, she rolled her good dress in her shawl. From a shelf she took her few things—a comb, a green ribbon, some stockings—and added them to the bundle.

As she slid down the ladder, Molly turned from the hearth and saw the bundle.

"Where are you going?"

"To An Marget's."

"Oh no, Mistress Smart! Your father said you go there no more. If you go, don't come back!"

"I won't!"

As she ran down the path she met Nancy coming along with Will. To her sister's sweet, wondering face, Jennet called, "Good-bye, Nan."

The wind was unusually warm and gusty, so the air was heavy with waiting. Above, clouds gathered, continually changing shape and company. Jennet went through the fields around Kynance, climbing hedge

94

walls rather than run through the village, for everyone to see the witch-girl with her wild eyes and streaming hair. On the Sabbath in Kynance Churchtown everyone would be out, chatting on doorsteps, the men playing games by the tavern, wrestling, and rolling the ball at the pins. Her father would be there.

She ran, walked, ran again, not thinking. But when she reached the path to Chelew, she slowed. What made her think An Marget would take her in? She'd not live at home any more, but the wisewoman had always lived alone.

Jennet stared at a robin hopping by the path and exclaimed, "Well, I don't know what else to do!"

The little redbreast flew up from the path and straightaway to Chelew. It was a good omen. Following, Jennet saw the bird fly into the open window of the cottage. Smoke wisped from the chimney, and a lamb and a kid scrambled up the hill behind the house. The door to Chelew stood open. Hesitantly, Jennet approached it and looked inside.

A man turned from the hearth. He was Captain Mathy Curnow, neat in Sunday dress.

"What are you doing here?" he said roughly.

She looked at him in surprise. "What are you? Where's An Marget?"

"Out." He frowned. "Go away, girl. Come back after tomorrow." And as she didn't move, he threw out his hands. "Go!"

She'd forgotten. Tomorrow, May Day, was also some special feasten-day for An Marget. The woman had told her to stay away. It was all too—nobody—where—? Jennet dropped down on the doorstone and cried out.

"But where shall I go?"

Her face twisted, tears blurred out the blustery face of the old man, and she began to sob violently—she, who almost never cried. She hid her face in her hands and twisted her body away as she sobbed, "Nobody—nobody—"

"Here. Get up out of the dirt."

Hands lifted her, firm but not rough. Uncle Mathy led her into the cottage and set her down on a stool in front of the fire. Clumsily, he dabbed a handkerchief at her wet face.

"Stop that infernal gibbering. What's the matter with you?" Despite his gruffness, Mathy's face softened into a kind squint.

Jennet told him of the quarrel, the decree, her flight. Her whispers were broken with sobs.

"But why the fuss?" he said, bewildered. "Why don't you stay home then? Why are you so determined to work for Marget?"

Jennet rubbed her hands across her cheeks, back to her neck. "I must!" she said, looking directly at Uncle Mathy. "I must learn what she knows."

He turned and poked at the fire. "Some things are

better not learned," he muttered. "Here, is it time to turn this cake?"

Jennet saw that he was tending a cake in a baking iron. And boiling in a pot hanging over the fire was a good piece of beef. She nodded, and then, glancing around, she saw that the room was decked out for a feast. There were fresh flowers in brass vases on the windowsills, and the table was covered with a fair white cloth. Fine dishes and silver were laid on the table, and food was set out—cheeses, honey, and bread.

Seeing her glance, Uncle Mathy exclaimed, "Oh, by tar, I suppose I'm going to tell you! Then maybe you'll take yourself off and leave this poor wisht woman to her foolish ways."

He got up and went to the door. "But first let me show you something. Come here."

Jennet followed him outside. But when she saw the man take the path that led up onto the cliffs above the sea, she stopped. It was the same way Marget had gone in her distress that night. Impatiently, Uncle Mathy motioned her to follow, putting a shushing finger over his mouth. When they had climbed the twists of the trail until they could see the open land on top of the cliff, he stopped and pointed.

"See them? There's Marget."

The moorland stretched wild and unhedged to the edge of the cliff, where it dropped abruptly to the ocean. Walking on the high land, Jennet saw three figures. They were a man and two women, all in the fine dress of lords and ladies. Jennet recognized the curved nose of An Marget, but Marget's hair was piled high, and she wore a ruffed and panniered gown of dazzling cloth. It was as surprising as seeing a queen and her courtiers strolling over the brambled moor. Slowly the group promenaded the cliff's edge, talking like old friends, while the gusty wind caught at ribbons and sleeves.

"What?" Jennet exclaimed.

"Ssh." The old man hushed her, urging her back down the path out of sight. "Come down before they see us."

In the cottage, he added furze to the fire, inspected the boiling beef, and raked the ashes around the baking iron.

"Fetch me a dram to drink, Jennet," he said. "This is hot work, and I've a windy tale to tell." He gave a nervous laugh.

Jennet hurried to bring Mathy the ale, and sat down on a stool. Both of them avoided sitting in An Marget's chair. At last she'd know Marget's secret. It was almost—presumptuous.

"Wait," she said, nervous too. She jumped up and got herself a mug of ale, then came back to the stool.

Uncle Mathy nodded in approval, took an appreciative sip from his own mug, and began. "Now,

Margaret came from a great family on the south coast beyond Penzance. I won't tell the name, for that's her will. I used to sail from that coast, and I knew of her by fame. As a girl she was a noted beauty, but she was strange even then, riding off by herself at times, hunting into odd corners of life. I'd see her at church, gliding with the grace of a bird. But her flashing eyes kept off her many suitors"—the old man's voice paced the story—"until she met Hugh C."

Jennet alerted. "Ah," she murmured.

"It should have been a fine meeting, for Hugh was of an ancient family that came over from Normandy with William the Conqueror."

"What?" Jennet interrupted. "What do you mean about a conqueror?"

"Drat, girl! Don't interrupt." Mathy rubbed his hand over his whiskers. "It was something long ago. . . . Where was I?

"Yes, Hugh C. When Hugh and Margaret met, it was like the striking of a sudden thunderstorm. Why not? Hugh was a fine devil of a man, she was a slash of moonlight. They fell in love. They danced together, they rode together, they walked the coast together. They pledged each other with gifts. He brought her soft leather gloves, she gave him a fine pair of knives.

"But it was all in secret, for Hugh was the black sheep of his family. He was a sailor—I sailed with him, and we were friends. When he was fifteen, Hugh ran away to sea, and by the time he was out of his teens, he was captain of a raiding ship."

"A pirate!" Jennet exclaimed.

He puckered his bushy brows at her. "We had better names for it. But Hugh's family disowned him for his wild ways, despite the riches he was gaining. And Marget's family would have nothing to do with him either. —What was that?"

Uncle Mathy sprang up and hurried to the door.

"I thought they were coming. I'd better shorten this tale, or they'll find you here. A drop more in my mug, if you please."

Jennet refilled his cup, and Uncle Mathy went on.

"So one fine night they ran away and were married. They sailed in his ship on a moonlight tide. I was along too. Marget and Hugh sailed together for two years, and I wish I had time to tell you the adventures we had."

Jennet mused with delight, "An Marget, married. Married to a pirate."

"Privateer! Then she came home to bear her lover's child. But it was a bad time, and I'll tell it quickly. Her family wouldn't take her in, and neither would his. So she went to live with old Betty Chyennis, down in a cove. Betty was the local white witch, and Marget had become friends with her in the days when she was exploring the countryside on her pony.

"Hugh promised to return before the child was born, but he didn't. Our ship was wrecked in a southern sea, and only I returned." Uncle Mathy rested his chin on his hand and stared into the fire. "I came back to tell Marget that my old friend was dead—her lover was drowned."

"Ohh."

"Coming on top of the cruel treatment of her family, the shock was too great. Despite the care of Betty Chyennis, Marget lost her child. For a while she was like a madwoman, and we feared she'd take her life. But she was tough. She raged that she had nothing left of Hugh but his love, and she'd make the most of that."

He sighed. "And aye, she has. Every year she keeps the feast of their wedding day, the first of May."

"So that's her feasten-day! Tomorrow. But, Uncle Mathy, that's beautiful!"

He shook his head. "You don't understand, girl. For thirty years Marget has loved no one but Hugh. It's not normal for a woman. It's twisted her. Thank the Lord, she stayed friends with me, for I'm the only one she relaxes with. But you see what she's done—become a white witch, full of fancies. She learned the business from old Betty Chyennis, and when Betty died, Marget came over here to start a new life. Jone and I followed, when I gave up the sea."

Jennet smiled at the old man. There was so much to

think about, but first, what a good, faithful friend he'd been to An Marget.

Then she said, "But An Marget has given her life to helping people, healing them. You said she's loved no one but Hugh. Maybe she's loved people that way."

"Hmph. Maybe. But you saw her last night, full of scorn. Nay, it's Hugh she still yearns for."

He glanced uneasily over his shoulder toward the door. Lowering his head to Jennet, he said in a husky voice, "She still hopes he'll come back."

Jennet stared at him.

"Him—or his ghost."

She remembered Malachai's voice on that fearful night. "He will come. I will come." Jennet's head jerked to look around the room. Where was the magpie?

The old man gripped her arms. "Sometimes she grows mad with yearning for him. That's why I warned you to take care of her." He let go of Jennet and shrugged sadly. "But you're only a girl. You can't. You should stay out of all this. Go home, Jennet, and marry some good boy. Don't go the way of a white witch."

Jennet tilted back her head. "But I—"

"Especially not with Margaret," he insisted. "She becomes wisht, and most so at the time of her wedding day. That's why those two people have come to keep the feast with her, to soften her sorrow and distract her. The man and woman walking the cliffs with Marget are old cousins who come to her at this time every year. She allows them because of their kindly intent. They lived in North Cornwall at the time she married Hugh C. and took no part in the hateful treatment her family dealt her."

Mathy poked at the beef. "Every year I tend their feast for them," he said. "Tonight and tomorrow we'll eat and tell tales and be merry. Maybe even dance a jig and sing 'Here's a health to the barley mow!' " He sighed. "Poor Marget."

Jennet got up and began to walk back and forth before the fire. Absently, she noticed the baking iron and pulled it from the ashes, for the cake must be well done by now. She paced, thinking over the tale.

While she walked, Uncle Mathy muttered, "But I don't like the coming of those cousins this year. She's been too eager for it. Before, she's tolerated them, but this year she could hardly wait. She's up to something."

Jennet stopped pacing. After all, old Mathy liked to make a good tale.

Impatiently she said, "What do you mean—something? You keep saying mad. An Marget is a good woman, just solitary. What does she do that's so mad?"

She remembered the woman running out into the night, but that was sorrowing, Jennet saw now, surely not madness.

Uncle Mathy threw out his hands. "Ah, it's all the ways she's wisht. For instance, look up over her bed.

You'll see a little window. Always she keeps it open, so that Chelew won't be closed to Hugh when he returns. So she can hear her lover's voice calling from the sea. So that Hugh's ghost can slip through it when he returns to her."

His voice grated on, making Jennet shiver, raising bumps on her arms. Ghosts. A spirit. An Marget wanting one to come—calling it.

Fearfully, Jennet stepped to the foot of the ladder that led up to the talfat. She hadn't noticed the window before. Slowly she climbed the ladder until her head was high enough. Yes, there was a small window cut in the stone wall. Its shutter was bound open, and she could see a patch of cloudy sky through the window.

A wry thought intruded. That would be a cold way to sleep on a winter's night, with an open window over your head.

Her eyes dropped to the oak bed under the window, and she gasped. At first, in the shadows under the roof, she thought there was a figure lying on the bed. Then she saw it was a suit of fine clothes laid out. On the pillow was placed a cocked hat. Next came a broad-skirted blue coat, with gold lace and bright anchor buttons. In the folds of the coat at the breast were white shirt ruffles, and rich lace hung out from the cuffs of the sleeves. Below, meeting the coat skirts, was a pair of high leather boots.

104

It must be the dress of her lover that Marget had laid out for her wedding day.

Jennet heard a sound in the gloom under the roof, and her eyes traveled further. Against the foot of the bed she saw a large oaken sea chest—and standing on it was the magpie, watching her.

With no movement but the opening of its beak, the bird said, "Go away." The voice issued effortlessly.

Jennet started, and in that instant her eyes took in view the foot of the bed. She saw the leather boots move together. Sparks jiggled before her eyes as she looked up the suit of clothing. Jennet shrieked, her grip loosened on the ladder, and she fell to the floor.

6

Jennet opened her eyes and stared up from the floor into Uncle Mathy's face.

"I saw him! I saw Hugh!" She twisted her head toward the talfat.

Uncle Mathy left off rubbing her hands and smacking her cheeks. "Nonsense." But a look of apprehension came over his face. He got up and climbed a few rungs of the ladder to look at the bed.

"Ho!" he blustered in relief. "Silly girl, all wrought up with my tale! There's nothing up there but his clothes. And that mournful magpie."

He went to the keg and pulled a mug of ale, shaking his head. "Don't know why she keeps that bird around. And teaching it to talk. Another one of her misguided ways. —Now then, drink this. It'll bring the color back to your cheeks."

He urged Jennet onto the settle to drink the ale and then made her take some broth of the beef. Jennet submitted, and the warm broth was welcome in her stomach, but she kept looking up to the talfat. Was it only the shadows above that had made the boots seem to move? Yet when she'd looked further, the chest of the coat had seemed filled out. She'd stopped short of the collar.

Uncle Mathy didn't give her time to think. Now he was trying to hustle her out of the cottage before Marget and the cousins returned. He'd cut off chunks of cheese and bread, and he thrust those at her, along with her bundle, which she'd dropped by the hearth.

"Here, go along home now like a good girl, Jennet. Mind my tale and forget Marget. Take another look at that Robin Pender. I've seen you eyeing the boy." He chuckled as he patted her shoulder and pushed her out the doorway.

There was no point in arguing. She wasn't wanted here. Jennet set off on the path back to Kynance. But at the stile over the hedge, where she could see the square church tower in the distance, she stopped and sat down on the stone step. Around her, the gorse bushes glowed with a luminous yellow as the late afternoon sun came from behind a cloud. Here in the shelter of the hedge the air was warm and sweet with the breath of the gorse blossoms. Idly, Jennet plucked at the ivy growing in the old stone wall.

Aloud she said, "Uncle Mathy is a silly old man. An Marget has more sense than he does."

At the sound of her voice, a meadow pipit sprang up from the hedge with an anxious peep. Jennet whistled the bird's cry after it and laughed once.

"I wouldn't hurt you, titlark. Fright. Foolish frights."

She couldn't go home now. She'd simply have to wait until the day after tomorrow to ask An Marget whether she would take her in. But where to wait? Jennet thought over the people in the village. There was Anne Pendower at the tavern, but they weren't really close friends. Besides, she didn't want to talk about it.

Jennet knew of a cave in the cliffs down the coast toward the giant's Logan Rock. She could wait there. Her stomach was content with beef broth and ale, and she had the bread and cheese Mathy Curnow had given her. She'd spend May Day by the sea, hunt for shells, watch the birds, let the wind blow through her hair.

Taking up her bundle, Jennet continued until she reached the footpath that led along the coast toward the Logan Rock and Penmorvah beyond. At the crossing, she stopped and looked up the narrow valley towards the Trevail cottage. In the distance, coming down from the woods around the millpond, she could see tiny figures bearing armloads of greenery. Those would be the women bringing home elder branches to ward off the witches tonight, Jennet thought, and a coolness came over her. She'd be spending May Day Eve alone on the cliffs.

Perhaps she'd better go home. After May Day she could go again to An Marget. But maybe she couldn't. She thought of her father's heavy anger. And there'd be Molly's mocking laughter if she came slinking home now. And Lovey's.

Jennet began to run along the coastal footpath. "Here's to the health of the barley mow," she sang loudly, to drown out thoughts. The wind caught at her hair and loosened the ribbon that bound it back. It was a storm-brewing wind, the kind witches would whisk on, astride their brooms.

Jennet stopped short and slapped her cheek. "Nonsense!" she cried. An Marget said that the flock of "witches" at Penmorvah were nothing but silly old women.

She left the footpath for a faint track that led over the headland toward the ocean. At least the cave was a familiar place. She had spent lazy afternoons in its shelter, looking out over the waves and daydreaming. The cliff here was a tumble of boulders and ledges as it dropped to the narrow rocky shore. In one of the niches a raven had its nest, and she'd grown fond of the bird, watching it from her cave. Stepping carefully down the rocks, Jennet descended toward the hollow in the cliff.

"Hi, Jennet, come and help!"

Below to the right she saw her half-brothers, Jemmy and Dick, busily chucking rocks at something below. It was the raven. The big black bird flapped and cawed on its nest on an unreachable ledge.

"Cry 'corpse' at me, you old devil!" Dick shouted, throwing another rock. "I'll make a corpse of you!" The stone grazed the bird's wing.

"Stop that!" Jennet cried.

"Say, Jennet," Jemmy called up to her, "we want to throw fire on the nest. Can you make the furze burn?"

"Yes," the older boy added. "Have you got anything to set a furze bush on fire? We're going to get one devil before night!"

The people along the coast had a fear of ravens, Jennet knew. Farmers shook their fists at the ominous black birds crying "corpse," and it was a common trick to throw fire on their nests. But she had never believed ravens were devils. From her cave she'd watched this bird mother her eggs. Once when a red fox had tried to climb down to the nest, the raven had flown over the fox, diving and trying to strike with her beak. The fox had stood still, head up and teeth showing, so that the raven could never land a blow. The raven had no special devil powers; yet when the bird had returned to its nest, defeated, the fox had loped away.

The wind stung salt on Jennet's face and ruffled the raven's lifted wing feathers. Little black heads bristled from the nest around the bird's body.

"You, Jemmy and Dick, come away from there!" Jennet ordered. "That bird is no devil. She's just a mother with young birds. I've watched her."

Jemmy peered down at the angry raven doubtfully, but Dick stopped with rock uplifted in his hand and stared at Jennet.

"You're a witch-girl. That's why you're protecting your devil-bird." He flung the rock at her instead.

Jennet dodged. "Molly's hunting you!" she cried. "If you don't go home quick, you'll both get a whipping."

Jemmy began to scramble up between the boulders, and after heaving one great rock at the nest, Dick followed reluctantly. From the top of the cliff he called down.

"You're going to fly with your raven tonight! Witch-girl!" Then he and Jemmy whirled and ran away, across the moorland.

Jennet clambered on down to the cave. The young fools. They'd believe anything, just like the rest of the villagers. At least there were some things she wasn't afraid of.

She sat down at the sandy entrance to the cave and watched the raven settle itself on the nest. She could just see the raven's ledge beyond a heap of stones. Below, the water swirled in white ruffles on the rim of shore and foamed high where the waves struck a rearing of jagged black rocks. The sun must have set, though the sky was too banked with clouds to tell. There was a yellowish-gray light over the ocean, and the expanse of water was a heaving gray blanket flecked with white. The wind was stronger now, bringing the smell of the sea and throbbing among the boulders louder than the shush of waves. Sand whipped Jennet's face, and she moved farther back into the hollow of the cliff, but even there the cold wind touched her. It promised a wild night for the eve of May Day.

In Penmorvah the old women would be gathering with An Katty Polteer. They might be silly old women, but Jennet had heard tales of An Katty's practices. With her ugly temper and sly ways, she was more of a black witch than a healing woman. They said she brewed with toads and baby fat, and people went to her for charms and advice when they wanted revenge on a neighbor. An Katty knew poisons, it was whispered. And she could raise the dead.

Jennet shuddered suddenly, picturing the black witch chanting up a spirit. Or whispering over a grave. An Marget had spoken scornfully of the witches of Penmorvah, "a flock of ignorant women, they," but An Marget had never mentioned their leader, An Katty, by name. Did she mean Katty Polteer was harmless too?

Jennet shook herself and turned to her bundle. Taking out the cheese, she broke off a piece and ate it to still her stomach. She smiled, thinking that by now

An Marget and the cousins, all in their fine dress, would be feasting and making merry. Perhaps right now Captain Mathy was shouting up a three-man's song. It would be a happy scene in the cozy cottage. That was the way to spend May Day Eve.

Not out in the cold, dreading witches.

The light had faded to near-darkness. Clouds hung over most of the sea, with only a faint rim of light at the horizon. She could see the whiteness of the waves spraying on the rocks, but her cliff companion, the raven on its nest, was obscured by darkness. Jennet felt the cave walls around her and strained to see into the black at the back of the hollow. She wished she had something to make fire with, as much for the light as the warmth.

When she'd eaten some of the bread, Jennet curled up on the sandy floor with her skirt tucked around her cold ankles, her head on the bundle. The sooner she slept, the sooner the night would pass. Her thoughts drifted to An Marget's love story—beautiful young girl and dashing sea captain, sailing on a moonlight tide. Margaret with creamy young cheeks and proud curved nose, eyes flashing with love . . . Hugh, broad-chested in a blue coat, striding the deck in those leather boots, dressed in the wedding clothes that lay on the bed— Jennet twitched her thoughts away from that. So far she'd been able to avoid picturing that. How had Marget's family been cruel to her? What had her father done? Jennet imagined him in a grand parlor, denouncing her, shoving her . . .

The wind hummed and rasped in clefts of the cliff; the waves throbbed against the shore. Gradually Jennet's pictures blended into dreams.

She woke with a start. What black hole was she in? The sound of waves . . . the cave. And something at the back of it. The sound again, a rustle. No points of light for an animal's eyes, but—a large, moving shape. Hugh's ghost was here!

Jennet screamed. She sprang up, tripped over the bundle, snatched it up out of her way, darted out to the rocks.

"No no no!"

She scrambled up the cliff in the darkness, falling over rocks, cutting her knees, tearing her hands. It's harder to climb rocks with shoes on, she thought, even as she shrieked, "No no, stay away!" A ghost could move so fast—was it looming over her back? Panting, she gained the top of the cliff and spurted forward. She tripped in a tangle of furze and fell, got up and ran on over the dark headland. At last, gasping, she looked behind her. She could see nothing in the close blackness of night.

Jennet ran and walked, stumbling and breathing hard. Gradually she began to wonder where she was going. Was there no refuge anywhere? She sobbed to herself, but as her panic subsided, she began to have

114

random thoughts. What time was it? Could this still be Sunday? It was Walpurgis Night, and here she was, out in the dark in the open country. She'd fled Hugh's ghost—or was it?—only to put herself at the mercy of the dark spirits that roamed the land. Jennet began to laugh harshly. You fool.

Abruptly she stopped. There was a ball of light in the distance. Up on the dim hills that rose from the headland was a yellow glow with streaks of red. It must be a May Day bonfire. Jennet ran toward the light.

When she reached the hill and began to climb upward through the brambles, she saw she was right. On top of the hill was a great bonfire, and against its flames she could see dark figures moving. Well then, she'd spend the night with the May Day watchers. It was better than being alone.

On the hilltop the fire was a red life roaring up into the night, spitting sparks up into the dark. Figures leapt and laughed as they gyrated around the fire in a circle. Some were dancing, and a voice cackled wildly. Jennet's heart jolted. It could be a witches' coven that she'd come upon, black witches meeting to celebrate the Devil. No, she recognized Dolly the Duck being handed around in the dance by Uncle Mathy's mate, Jack Tregear. For all their wild gyrations, these were Kynance folk.

Jennet ventured to the edge of the hilltop and sat down on a stone in the shadows. Against the bonfire, silhouettes of legs and arms flung out in the dance; flame light flickered on faces, so that it was hard to know people. Faces lit, leered, and were gone in shadows. Someone scraped out fast music on an old fiddle; some shouted the beat of the song, others drank from mugs. Mugs passed from hand to hand in bursts of laughter, and there were many visits to the keg. No one seemed to notice Jennet on her stone. She found she was still clutching her bundle and dropped it beside her.

The gusty wind on the open hilltop whipped the bonfire and made it crackle furiously. Clouds blew low. As a gray wisp scudded overhead, it lit red with the glow of the fire, and a man lifted his mug to the cloud.

"There goes an old witch now!" he shouted. "Singed her skirt tail. Drop a little lower, witch, and we'll burn you!"

People laughed, shouting, "Burn the old witch!"

Dolly the Duck squawked with laughter. "Singed her skirt tail, hey!"

Jennet's mouth twisted. They were brave enough, with a fire and a fiddle and a keg of ale. The dancers leapt on around the flames to the music. Jennet saw Nancy's Will whirling with a girl, but she wasn't Nan. The girl was a stranger, perhaps from over Penmorvah way. Will must be having himself a last fling before he wed. Jennet recognized that none of the steadier family people of Kynance were here. Then she saw Robin

Pender. He was clasping hands in the dance with a girl who was another stranger. She had yellow hair that gleamed brassy in the firelight, and she wore a bright green skirt which flounced above her knees as she skipped. As she flung back her head and laughed up at Robin, her white teeth caught the light. He laughed down at her, eyes only on her.

Jennet jumped up and pushed through the folk around the keg. Finding an empty cup, she drew a dram and drank some of it, choking at its sweet fieriness. This was stronger stuff than ale that they were drinking—honey mead. Her insides rushed with warmth as she turned to watch the dancers, her eyes searching the flickers of firelight and shadow. There they were, still laughing.

Oh, I wish I were laughing and leaping!

She became aware that people near the keg were looking at her and muttering. Then a woman exclaimed, "Go off, Jennet Trevail! You're not wanted here."

Jennet stumbled as someone jostled her from behind, and mead splashed on her skirt.

"The witch-girl!" went up the cry.

"A witch, right in our midst!"

"Witches? Where?"

Trying to make her hand steady, Jennet lifted the mug and sipped the mead while she stared back at the folk who had drawn away from her.

"The evil eye!" That was Dolly's quack.

The fiddle music stopped with a screech, and the dancers turned to see the commotion. Jennet stood with her back to the dark, trying to stare down the pointing fingers and shouts. In the midst of the noise, the words sounded.

"Burn the witch!"

Instantly, as she flinched, Robin Pender was at her side.

"Jennet's no witch. She's with me. Fiddler, where's your music. Earn your drink!"

Thunder rumbled in the distance.

"Aye, let's dance before the storm," shouted Jack Tregear.

Feebly, the whine of the fiddle began and then speeded to a vigorous lilt. Knocking aside Jennet's cup, Robin grasped her hands and swung her into the dance around the bonfire. Whirling, Jennet glimpsed a cluster of folk watching her, and then she forgot them, as she looked up at Robin's face. He was looking down at her with intensity, not laughing.

Attempting a smile, she said, "And you? Aren't you afraid of me?"

He grinned, and his eyes were flecked with firelight. "Just enough."

Hands clapped out the pulse of the fiddle; voices shouted the song. Robin clasped his hands on Jennet's waist and whirled her with the music.

"Jennet, Jennet, Jennet Trevail!" he sang.

Jennet skipped to the beat, warm and breathless. "What about the girl—the one you—danced with?"

He laughed down at her, not looking away from her. "She's just someone who was here."

Lightning tore a white rift in the black sky over the moor nearby, thunder boomed, and the dance sped faster. The music and the mead sang in Jennet's ears. Firm in Rob's hands, she spun, laughing, tossing her hair.

"Rob, Rob-Bob!" She sang grace notes to his "Jennet, Jennet, Jennet!"

Breathless, they stopped when the music stopped, still looking at each other. Jennet saw Robin's face, suddenly illuminated by a glare of lightning, and then great drops of rain began to fall.

"Come along!" Robin pulled her away from the fire.

"Where?"

"To shelter!"

Jennet remembered to snatch up her bundle, and they ran into the dark, over the moor. Robin's cottage—An Sarah's—was not far away, he said. Lightning flashed around them; the rain on the wind chased them as they blew before it, laughing, but they reached the stone farmhouse before the storm of rain fell.

Inside, Robin built up the fire in the hearth and turned to Jennet, where she stood trying to get her breath back. Smiling, he thrust his hands through her black hair.

"Your hair is like cloud wisps blowing over the moon. Come, my wild-haired girl, sing to me."

Lightly he tugged her down before the hearth, and the firelight made his eyes dance even more. What was it about his eyes, that they seemed to hold all his spirit? Jennet sang, "Hey nonny, maids-o! On the first of May Day!" Then she sang a ballad of the sea, and her voice softened, thinking of Margaret and Hugh. Robin put a hand up to her hair to smooth it back.

"Have you ever wanted to go to sea?" she asked him.

"No, I'm a farmer," he said, watching her. "I'd stay home with my wife."

Jennet looked down, her face warmer than the fire warranted.

"But I would like to see more than this piece of coast," Robin added, sitting up and crossing his legs. "Have you ever been out of sight of the smoke of your own chimney, Jennet?"

She nodded. "But only in wandering the moors and coast," she said, "and to St. Ives. I'd like to see the south coast and Penzance someday."

"I've been to Penzance!" he said. "And I've climbed St. Michael's Mount that rises out of the waters of the bay."

Eagerly he described the conical mountain with its

castlelike monastery on top. Jennet listened in fascination.

"And Jennet, there's another wondersome place in our west of Cornwall. Did you know we live near Land's End? The end of the land of all of Britain!"

Of course she'd heard of the place. Land's End lay on beyond Penmorvah and St. Just, lonely crags of rock jutting into the sea at the end of Cornwall.

"Yes," she said, smiling at his enthusiasm. "I'd love to see the place."

"From Land's End the ocean stretches clear away to the New World. We could stand and look over the water—Jennet, let's go there tomorrow!"

It would be a long day's walk, he said, but they were both strong. And they could spend the night at his brother's house in Penmorvah on the way back.

"A May Day jaunt!" Jennet cried. "Oh aye, I'll come with you, Robin!"

He leaned over and touched her mouth with his finger, and his eyes were gay in the firelight. "How far?" He kissed her mouth.

"Oh!"

Robin drew her into his arms and looked down at her. The lean lines of his face weren't laughing now. "How far will you come with me, Jennet?"

Wide-eyed, she looked at his tawny face, the golden curl by his ear, so near her lips. She wanted to touch the curl of hair with her lips. Instead, he kissed her again, warm mouth on hers, strong arms holding her close, and it was like the sweet fire of mead running through her. The fire hummed and popped, whispering ease. Her lips moved against his—no! Jennet jerked away, shaking her head violently.

He reached to pull her back, whispering, "Jennet, why not?"

"I'm not fit!" she blurted.

He laughed softly. "Ah, little Jennet."

"I'm apprenticed for a witch!"

"Give it up," he whispered, eyes sparkling.

Why not? With golden Rob couldn't she be safe from the dark? His strong arms, his laughter—

"What did you mean, 'laugh with God'?" She watched the man in the firelight, intent on his answer.

"Ah, who knows?" He shrugged, smiling. "Jennet, come here."

"Tell me," she urged.

Robin spread out his broad farmer's hands and looked down at them. "God is good. He must laugh. I laugh with him."

Jennet stared from his face to his hands, trying to make something of his answer, trying to make a talisman. It wasn't enough. If there was something there, she didn't understand it.

She moved over to the side of the hearth and lay down to sleep, pulling her skirt over her feet. She wished he weren't watching. She wanted to cry.

"Good night, Robin," she said.

The fire whispered. After a moment, Robin said, "Go up to An Sarah's bed. I'll stay here."

Jennet climbed the ladder to the talfat. She shuddered at sleeping in the bed where the woman had died, but she didn't trust herself to be near Robin now.

Lying under the blanket on the pallet, she listened to his movements below. He was scraping up the ashes, banking the fire, going to the door to check the latch. Rain poured down on the thatched roof close over her head; thunder rumbled once in the distance. If they were married, he'd come up to bed now, and they'd lie together, sheltered from the storm. She heard something clang below. Had he kicked out in anger? The bench creaked as he threw himself down on it.

I can cry now, Jennet thought. But she didn't. She lay dry-eyed, staring up into the shadows buttered by the firelight. She loved Robin Pender. For an instant she let herself know it, with all the burst of a wave against a cliff. Then the pain of it broke and spattered. She could never be Robin's. Yes, he would come to her if she called. Right now, if she called over the edge of the talfat, he'd come up to her. Scared face and all, he'd chosen her. Jennet's hands twisted the edge of the blanket.

But loving Robin wasn't enough. He couldn't protect her. He couldn't laugh away demons.

Only when she was a white witch could she protect herself. A white witch like An Marget was remote and powerful, a dedicated priestess to magic for the sake of overcoming evil—and how could a woman like that be a wife!

Turning on her side, Jennet drew up her knees and covered her face with her hands. She was unfit for a loving wife. From childhood she'd been marked out, either for the Devil to use, or as a white witch—to combat the powers of evil.

Again she saw the wedding clothes of the sea captain, laid out on Marget's bed. In the shadows she saw the silent magpie with its inner voice. She saw the polished leather of the tall boots and how the boots moved.

"No," she whimpered. "Why should I—"

Maybe she had run from nothing in the cave. The thoughts came, disjointed. There were lots of things other people feared that she didn't. "I'll teach you to sort out the nonsense," An Marget had said. Gracey Winkey and her fears, that was nonsense. Yet even Gracey could forget her fears and be a wife.

Jennet flung herself onto her back again. She lay listening to the sound of the rain beating on the thatch over her head; then she let out an emptying sigh. She named it clearly to herself.

We all fear the dark. But I *see* the spirits.

Maybe there'd been nothing in the cave tonight,

but she'd seen those boots move. She hadn't imagined that night long ago, when she'd lain beside Sarah Polgrain's cold body and the shadows took shapes. A demon must have entered her then, chinking open her mind ever since. Grandma'am should have had her exorcised. Jennet's mouth twisted in a bitter smile. She could see the fluster Piggy Thomas would go into if he were asked to exorcise anything, fluttering his hands, snorting, fussing.

But An Marget could understand. An Marget would teach her the powers of a white witch. When she was Jennet, White Witch of Kynance, she could bind and banish any spirit that appeared—she could rid herself of the demon.

Her eyes ached with dryness, but she stared up into the shadows until the drumming of the rain softened and died away. Then she slept.

7

Jennet woke with last night's thoughts clinging like greasy cobwebs. She'd spent the night where An Sarah had died. Had Marget seen Hugh's ghost? How the flames of the bonfire had leaped! Robin Pender must be disgusted with her now. He must be awake, for she heard sounds below.

To wash away the thoughts, Jennet opened the small window of the talfat and leaned out into the early morning air. The storm had left a fresh-washed sky, and through a dip in the hills she caught a glimpse of the sea—a shimmering mist of blue, like another sky laid out at the edge of the land. Jennet breathed in the soft air. It was just past dawn, and birds were filling the air with lilts and trills. Near the house, a clump of hawthorn trees was luminous with white blossoms against the blue sky. The day was so sweet anyone coming upon it unexpectedly would know it was the first day of May. It was a day just made for journeying out to see new sights.

Jennet smoothed her dress and climbed down the ladder. The windows below were open, and Robin was boiling eggs in a kettle over the hearth. He kept the cottage neat, she noticed—slate floor freshly brushed.

Rob turned to her, and he was smiling. "Haven't I made a fine day for our jaunt? You didn't know I was a conjurer. That's a cut above a witch, you know."

He grinned, and Jennet flushed. His hair gleamed as if he'd rubbed a wet towel over it.

"Eggs for nooning," he added, indicating the kettle, "and we'll take plenty of cheese and bread."

Jennet clasped her hands at her waist and looked down at them. Why not? Nothing could make it any harder for her to forget Robin now. She'd have this one May Day with him.

"All right, Robin Pender, I'll come along with you!" She was surprised to hear her voice come out lilting like the birdsong.

While Robin let the cows out of the shed to the pasture and fed the chickens, Jennet cooked the breakfast porridge. Leaving it to simmer in the pot, she dug in her bundle until she found a fresh green ribbon to bind back her hair. Her father had brought it to her long ago, his face soft—not harsh as it had been when he'd thrown her against the table. That day he'd

127

brought Lovey and Nancy blue ribbons, but hers had been different, shining green, deeper than the green of the fields in spring.

Jennet had noticed a polished silver mirror hanging on the wall—really, An Sarah had lived most comfortably, such a pleasant cottage—and she looked in the mirror to adjust the ribbon. The green was glossy against her dark hair, and her eyes looked startlingly blue in contrast to the green.

"All round-eyed, ready for your May Day jaunt," she said, laughing at herself.

Robin came in whistling, and they sat down to the porridge. As they ate, he chatted simply as a friend, with no hint of last night's passion, and Jennet was relieved. This was no day for worry.

It was a day of sparkle and glow, dew sparkling on the neat green fields around Robin's house, hawthorn and gorse blossoms glowing against the soft sky. As Robin and Jennet set off, her spirits sparkled to match the day, and she sang out in reply to a passing bird. Robin whistled along with her. Jennet ran a few steps out of eagerness, and she and Rob struck off over the moor toward the coastal footpath. Below them the sea lay calm as a summer ocean, mist still rising from the water in the early morning.

At first they passed through known territory. Jennet had been to Penmorvah on a few occasions, though the village itself held no attraction for her. It was a village of strangers. Beyond Penmorvah they took a shortcut that Robin knew about. The path rose inland over the hills in a diagonal toward Land's End. Most of the way would be new to Rob, too, for although he said he'd been to Land's End once as a boy, he'd taken the long way around the coast. That time he'd gone to a wrestling match in St. Just, and then he and the men had walked on to the end of the land—to say they'd been there.

Still near Penmorvah, they passed a great house with stone outer walls, and Jennet paused near the gate to peer into the courtyard. She'd heard of this place, Tregwarra, and the family. It was the only great house on the north coast, and Jennet was amazed at its grandeur, an even more impressive building than Kynance Church. She studied the broad front of granite blocks, the gabled roof, and the turrets of chimney stacks. Above the arched doorway was a roofed balcony supported on pillars, and on either side were mullioned windows of glass. Beyond the house, Jennet glimpsed other stone buildings, gardens, and the rise of a tower with pigeons flying in and out the slits at the top.

As they walked on, Robin amused Jennet with tales of the family and how one of the fine ladies had played the clown at the midsummer celebrations. Robin had never roamed beyond the house in this direction, so presently he and Jennet shared the delight of being adventurers in a new land. They came upon a long snakelike stone hedge winding away inland. It was unusually high and overgrown with turf and furze, and the stones were more closely fitted than in most hedges. The wall looked so ancient that Jennet speculated it could have been built by Boclas to mark his lands off from the next giant's kingdom.

"Could be." Robin laughed. "Tell it that way, and you can start a new tale."

The land rose higher into the sky. They came upon a badger going down to earth and a heron fishing in a stream, long neck bent, intent at its work, but not a human did they see.

Then came open, barren moorland, and one stunted hawthorn tree scraping its dead branches against the sky.

Robin pointed to the twisted limbs. "There's a witch for you," he said, chuckling.

Crone-humped back, black grasping arms . . . Jennet stared at the tree. Last night in her panic, if she'd come upon this twisted shape looming out of the darkness, she would have been sure it was a black witch. Especially as witches were said to turn themselves into hawthorn trees on Walpurgis Night. Yet now in the sunny day anyone could see it was only a tree . . . Though, her thoughts ventured, last night it might have been a witch . . . Stop that, Jennet told herself sternly. Is every dead tree to be a witch?

As they walked the faint path, Jennet was quiet

with the silence of the wide moor country. Then she said to Robin, "You're not afraid, are you? I mean, of witches and demons."

He smiled. "Not often. I'm just God's fool, I guess."

"What do you mean?"

"Well"—he shrugged—"I trust Him."

Jennet thought about that. Just like that, he trusted. It sounded good under the blue sky, with birds springing up from the heath.

She said, "You know how people tell tales of seeing witches and piskies, demon dogs and the like— Do you ever see creatures of God on earth? Nobody ever talks about seeing angels."

Rob looked down at her, his green eyes flecked with light. "I see one now."

"No, really." She giggled. *I, Jennet—giggling!*

Robin looked around as he strode over the moor. "Yes, I see God's creatures. That lark, flying, the badger we saw. And all the works He's made—hills and sea, sunrises and that leaf of bracken."

He scooped up a stone and tossed it, turning to her and laughing. "Why fret about an occasional demon, girl, when God's works are all around you!"

Jennet couldn't help laughing. And yet—God had made Gracey Winkey too. Also, hills and seas weren't the same as spirit creatures. She couldn't picture God or see Him walking on earth. Well—

"What of Jesus Christ?" she said.

"What about Him?" Then Robin looked shame-faced. "Christ our Savior," he mused. "Yes, He was here. He made the lame to walk, the blind to see. He heals all things to wholeness."

Robin's answers were so simple and trusting. Jennet pulled off a frond of bracken and unfolded the new curl of leaf.

Boldly she said, "If He can do that, why doesn't He? Why doesn't He walk the earth now and forever, making all things whole?"

Robin glanced at her. "I don't know. Maybe He wants us to do it."

Jennet was silent, thinking. Her head down, she noticed a green feather of moonwort on the ground. It was a small fern that An Marget had been wanting just the other day.

"Aha!" Jennet exclaimed. She plucked up the moonwort and put it in her pocket. Suddenly it occurred to her that a white witch's healing helped make creatures whole. "Ha!" she cried in delight. She was in tune with God's scheme. "All right, Robin!"

He pulled his mouth down in mock dismay at her series of exclamations. "Who knows what goes on in the minds of women? Wondersome creatures!"

"We'll never get there at this rate!" Jennet exclaimed happily.

She began to run, and Robin raced after her. The

sun was high, the land warm, and they rested on the bracken in a thicket of gorse. Jennet leaned back, sucking the sweetness of a yellow blossom. She felt as easy as a flow of honey, drowsy with the buzz of bees flying about the blue flowers of some sheep's-bit nearby. Something passed at the edge of her eye, and she murmured, "Something lovely just flew by, golden drift of butterfly."

Butterflies were like God's fairies.

Robin leaned over her, tickling her cheek with a spray of gorse. Laughing, Jennet leaped up and sprang away, singing, and Rob bounded down the hill after her. They came upon hawthorn trees mounded white with bloom, and Robin tucked a creamy blossom under the ribbon in her hair.

"Turnabout!" Jennet wound a wreath of blossoms and thrust it on Rob's head, and they ran on, laughing at their foolishness. Around a curve of hill they startled a shepherd and his sheep. Rob wore his wreath proudly past the man, and then when they were out of sight, they laughed harder. "Ah, Rob-Bob!" Jennet gasped.

At last, they came over another hill and saw the land dropping away to a rim of cliffs and the ocean sparkling beyond.

"Land's End!" Robin said. "We've come to the end of the world!"

"And there will be an old woman at a well who will grant our every wish!"

They hurried down and over the tableland and finally stood on the edge of the cliffs with the wind rushing over them even on this soft May Day. All was rock and water here at the end of creation, rocky buttresses jutting out into the sea, waves lashing at their base, gnarled rocks thrusting out of the white-flecked waves farther out from land. And then nothing but water stretching away to the southwest.

"There," Robin pointed, "beyond where we see, is the New World. If we sailed for months, we'd come to another great land."

It was as if he saw a path over the water.

"Would you like to go there?" Jennet couldn't imagine another shore so far away.

"I might." He stood looking over the ocean that went on and on.

Jennet shivered in the wind. He'd said he was a farmer.

"Let's eat," she said. "I'm starved."

They climbed partway down the cliff to be on the very last of the land and found amongst the rocks a grassy place sprinkled with sea pinks. As they ate their bread and eggs and cheese, the waves beat and swirled around the rocks below. A gull came to examine them, and Jennet tossed crumbs to the bird.

He's from the New World, it pleased her to imagine, come clear across the sea to share our bread!

Then they climbed around the grassy cliffs, and

Jennet gathered small flowers and pebbles as souvenirs. She thought, In future years when I am a white witch, I'll look at these and remember the day I went to Land's End with Robin Pender. They had the place all to themselves, not a person or a house in sight. For a long time they rested on a cliff shelf while they stared at the waves that kept coming from the New World to beat on the rocks off Land's End. But the sun was well past noonday, and at last they started their journey homeward.

As they walked toward the hills, Robin told Jennet the tale of how King Arthur had fought off invading Danes near Land's End. The Sea Kings had landed and marched north, spreading destruction, but Arthur and his knights met them and gave battle.

"The slaughter was so terrible they say the mill was worked with blood that day," Robin said.

Not a Dane who'd landed remained alive. The few men left in charge of the ships tried to flee, but a holy woman brought home a west wind by emptying the Holy Well against a hill and sweeping the church from the door to the altar. The ships couldn't sail away but were dashed by the wind against the rocky shore. Thus perished the last great army of Danes who dared to land on Cornish shores, Robin said.

Around the curve of coast was the village of Sennen, he said, and there King Arthur and nine other kings had pledged their victory with water from St.

Sennen's Well. A great feast was made at Table-men, and Merlin, the prophet, declaimed a poem defying invaders.

Jennet looked over the quiet land that might once have been a battleground. "How awful!"

Robin's storytelling voice dropped to his usual banter. "Well, you women have your spirits, and we men have our gore."

She smiled at him. "That's not very funny."

"And I shouldn't make fun of you, for I may need to have truck with spirits myself," he added cheerfully.

Her eyes jerked around to him, and he met them with a serious look.

"Jennet, you were right last night to resist me. You want marriage, not a night's fancy."

Jennet shook her head, but he went on.

"I want to marry you, Jen, witch-girl." Robin paused as he looked at her, his mouth softening— "But I must have a place to bring you home and the means to support you."

The problem was his lost savings and the question of who was to inherit from An Sarah Pender. Before she died, An Sarah had hidden everything away, her will, her gold and his savings along with her own. Once, the old aunt had shown Robin her will, and he was to inherit everything she had—cottage, land, and sack of money—but now, though he'd searched the cottage, he couldn't find the will.

"I can't stay on the farm much longer. Without the will, the rest of the Penders have just as much right to the place as I do. I earned money working for a Penmorvah farmer, but now that's disappeared too. I haven't a penny to buy bread for you, Jennet."

"What a backhanded proposal." She tried to laugh, but the words and the laugh came out awkwardly. She turned and looked back at the last glimpse of the sea off Land's End. Eyes on the distant water, she said, "I'm sorry for your trouble—truly—but I can't marry you anyway. You know that I'm set to be a white witch."

The wind from the sea made a lonely sound on the moor, and the day dimmed as a small white cloud floated over the sun. Robin touched Jennet's hand and pulled her around to look at him.

"Couldn't you do both? Marry me and heal people from our cottage—if I ever have a cottage."

Jennet stared at him—such loving eyes looking at her. She must never admit she loved him.

Jerking her hand away, she cried, "It wouldn't be the same! A white witch does more than heal with herbs. There are mysteries."

She'd echoed An Marget, she realized. You don't want a wife who sees spirits, she thought. Though if she told him that, he might only laugh. Then she thought desperately, maybe he *can* laugh it away, and she said, "Robin, I see spirits."

But he didn't laugh. He looked at her, then turned

and began walking along the dirt track over the moor, motioning her to follow.

"I wish you could see An Sarah's spirit and ask her where her will is," he muttered.

Jennet hurried after him. She couldn't tell whether he was joking.

He said suddenly, "Would you know spells to find lost things? Have you learned that much?"

"No," Jennet said, frightened. How did he see her, really? She didn't dare tell him the rest, how demons possessed her mind.

"Never mind." His head came up as he strode on. "I have a plan. I haven't told you all. An Katty Polteer in Penmorvah can work wonders. I'm going to ask her to help me find the will. Or at least my savings. When I've got that back, I won't leave you alone, Jennet Trevail, until you promise to marry me!"

"What! What do you mean about An Katty?"

"Why, she's the smartest witch in these parts," Robin said, glancing at her in surprise. "I'll get her to help me."

"She's nothing but an ignorant old woman!" Jennet cried.

"Nay," he said stubbornly, "she knows powerful charms. She has a glass. She sees things in it."

Jennet's body chilled as she listened to Robin. He said he knew An Katty could work bad deeds, but he'd have nothing to do with her wickedness. He'd only ask her to look in the ball of glass and see where An Sarah had put his sack of savings and the will.

Jennet felt chilled through. Her bones were made of icicles. Robin Pender was no wiser than the rest, for all his laughing with God. He'd put his trust in a black witch.

She tried once more. "Consult An Marget," she begged. "Not only is she wiser, but she's a good woman."

Robin smiled at her. "Faithful apprentice. But she's not wiser. I've lived in Penmorvah all my life, and I know An Katty's power."

The day was ruined. Trust in God's works! Jennet thought bitterly. There was even more pain when Rob teetered through a bog to fetch her some pink spikes of bogbean flowers, and watching him, she found she still loved him. He tried to tease her into laughter, but the delight of the morning was lost. The afternoon dulled with gathering clouds, and the way back to Penmorvah was long. When they passed Tregwarra, cattle near the great house were lowing for their evening milking. By now Jennet's legs were so tired she felt the effort of moving one ahead of the other. When they reached Penmorvah, the sun had set unnoticed in a mist of clouds over the ocean. The bright May Day had settled into a heavy evening.

"We'll sup at Tom's and then go to see An Katty," Robin said.

139

"What? Tonight?"

"Why not? The sooner the better, love!"

"Well, I won't go with you!" Jennet declared.

He smiled at her uncertainly, saying, "I don't understand you, Jennet," but he seemed determined to follow his plan.

Robin's brother's house was a small stone cottage just like the Trevail cottage, full of smoke and the crowding of people. Studying Rob's brother, Jennet saw a thickset older man, perhaps thirty, with sandy hair. He had none of Robin's shine, though there was a like cast to the straight noses of the brothers. Tom's wife, Mary, was a sharp-voiced woman with hair straggling down the sides of her face, who ran to and fro after a rabble of young children. The family looked tired from their May Day festivities and not pleased to find visitors on the doorstep.

However, Mary eyed Jennet shrewdly, and Jennet knew what she was thinking. No girl journeyed with a man on May Day to Land's End, as Robin happily announced they'd done, if she was simply a friend.

Grudgingly, Mary scraped out the bottom of the kettle for them, and when they'd eaten, Robin said he'd step out for an hour on an errand. Jennet was sore with Mary's sharp looks and the noise of the children. She didn't want to stay here alone with these unfriendly strangers. Besides, she'd been thinking about the black witch. Despite fear and disgust, a more salty sensation had been growing in her. She was just plain curious to see An Katty Polteer.

"Thank you," Jennet said to Mary and slipped out the door after Robin into the dusk.

"I thought you weren't coming," he said in surprise.

"Well, I came out with you to see the sights. Might as well see them all." Jennet laughed in spite of everything.

Robin shook his head. "Women!"

But he wasn't very aware of her just now. In the graying light, Jennet saw his face grow serious. They passed Penmorvah's mean little church, and Jennet thought, Our church is prouder. And we have bells, Peter and Paul. Quickly she prayed, *Jesus Christ, protect us tonight*. Even she knew it was better to put your trust in God than in a black witch. She felt stronger than Robin.

He led the way to a cottage on the edge of the village. It was gray and squatty in the dusk but no different from the other houses except that the dirt dooryard looked a bit scruffier. At the side of the house grew a few brambles of garden. The place was closed up for the night, but cracks of lights showed through the shutters. Robin knocked.

After a wait, the door swung open on a smoky, dark room. There was no one standing inside, but Jennet couldn't help gasping. The first thing she saw was a wicked stuffed beast hanging from the rafters, like a swollen snake with short legs. Its long jaws gaped with fangs; it had a scaly body and long tail.

"Enter, Robin Pender. I've been expecting you," said a voice in short wheezes.

An old woman stepped from behind the door. She wheezed a chuckle and suddenly thrust a gnarled finger first at Robin's face, then Jennet's, then pointed it to the hanging beast.

"That's a crocodile," she said, crackling out the syllables. "He's a devil-beast from a devil-land. My sweet Pommy."

Jennet shuddered as the woman reached up and stroked the snout of the creature.

"Old Marget's magpie is nothing beside you, Pommy—is it, love!" The old woman stroked the thing, then hitched herself around abruptly to glare at Jennet. "Come to learn my secrets, hey?"

Jennet drew back against Robin.

The woman cackled. "Oh, I know all about you, Jennet Trevail, how you're An Marget's girl." The words came in short breaths. "You'd do better to come to me."

Jennet stared at An Katty Polteer, ancient woman hunched in black shawl and black skirt. The only live thing about her was the gleam of her eyes under squinted eyelids in a face puckered with wrinkles. She was dirty. Jennet was accustomed to dirt, but this was old dirt grimed into the wrinkles, clotted on the shawl, smeared down her skirt. Yet she only matched the filth of her cottage. It was littered with trash; overturned pots had spilled food on the floor, and there was a sour smell to the place. A weak fire sputtered in the fireplace hole, sending out wisps of smoke, and only one candle was lit on the table. From the corner there came a sudden snort and then loud snores. In the shadows, Jennet saw a man sprawled asleep against a bench. He was drunk, Jennet decided.

"Heh, that's my old lutterpooch," An Katty said, chuckling. "Tammy, he did have a fine May Day!"

At the sound of his name the old man roused and hiccoughed. His voice blared out of sleep, "Devil take me, if I don't whack—" and muttered off into snores again.

"Lutterpooch" was right, Jennet thought. Tammy Polteer was a lazy sloven if she ever saw one.

An Katty hitched herself over to the table in a quick, sideways walk, motioning her guests to follow.

"Come sit down with me, Robin Pender," she wheezed. "I know what you've come for."

Robin glanced at Jennet. See how smart she is, his eyes said. Jennet stayed by the door, but Robin sat down at the wooden table, opposite the old woman, being careful to keep his sleeves out of a puddle of gravy. He started to speak to An Katty, but she thrust her twisted finger over his mouth. Jerking forward, she stared into Robin's eyes; then her head drooped. Her voice took on a low croon.

"You've come to find lost things. An Sarah has hidden your money and her will."

Everyone knows that, Jennet thought. An Katty looked and acted exactly as everyone expected a black witch to. And because of that, strangely, Jennet found she was less frightened than she'd expected to be—despite the old woman's abrupt movements and the fanged crocodile. She watched Robin to see if he was being taken in. He in turn was watching An Katty closely as she pulled a small ball of glass from somewhere in her skirt. Nodding and whispering, the old woman polished the ball with a corner of her shawl, and a gleam of candlelight flashed off the glass. An Katty placed the crystal on the table between her and Robin. It sparkled clean and bright amidst the dark filth of the room.

"See how clear it is?" An Katty said, and Robin nodded. "Place your hands over it."

He did.

Then she chanted, "Glass doth darken, glass doth show, glass doth tell all he know."

She muttered some foreign syllables and breathed heavily on the glass ball. As the moisture cleared, Robin sucked in his breath. Jennet started forward to see. There were lines and shadows in the glass. They moved—

"I see a mound, a long hump of earth. I see a tree, great yew tree. It is An Sarah's grave near the tree. She is calling to you, Robin Pender. She has something to tell you."

As the old woman whispered, Jennet backed away in fear that swelled in her throat as if it would choke her. The glass had changed. Under An Katty's influence the pure glass had changed to show pictures. An Katty was not just an ignorant old woman playacting. She did have power, power that could swirl up forces of darkness and—

An Katty was saying the most shocking thing of all. "We must raise An Sarah's spirit and ask her where the lost things are."

In harsh pants of breath she told Robin how she would raise the dead, according to the dead woman's desire. Jennet cowered against the fireplace wall, trying not to hear. She looked once at Robin, hoping he'd laugh, but his face was intent on the old woman, and she couldn't see his eyes.

"Raise the dead," he muttered. "No, old woman, I don't like that. Can't the ball tell you—"

"Nay, stop!" An Katty hissed. "Sarah Pender doth call you from the grave! She cannot rest. I warn you, Robin Pender, do not refuse her, or her spirit may roam back to her house to search . . ." The whisper went on in the dark room.

Robin propped his elbows on the table, unmindful

of the dirt, and drooped his head on his hands.

Don't listen, Jennet willed. *Come away.*

A gust of wind rattled the shutters, and the door, not fully closed, was flung open. The dying fire flared, and there was movement under the shadowed rafters. To Jennet's horror, the crocodile swayed in the rush of wind, its fanged snout retreating, advancing. Jennet ran to the door and pushed it shut to stop the movement of the devil-beast.

"All right, we'll do it," Robin said in a low voice. "When—"

"First you must give me five shillings," An Katty said rapidly. "I must have the money to buy drugs, rare spices and ores, to protect us from evil influences around the spirit."

Robin protested that he had no money, that he would pay her when his savings were found, but the old woman insisted she must have the shillings now. He could get them from his brother. Tom earned good money as a tin miner, she said. He'd have some silver saved up, and Robin could soon repay him when his sack of savings was found. At last, under her urgings, Robin agreed.

An Katty panted and nodded her black-shawled head until wisps of hair escaped around her face. "You won't regret it, Robin Pender. Tomorrow I'll send my old Tammy to St. Ives with the shillings to buy what we need. When he returns, we'll go to Sarah Pender's grave, you and I. On the third night from now we will raise the dead!"

On the third day He rose again from the dead. Jennet remembered the words they said in church. *Jesus, protect us.* She said the words in the way she used to touch the holed stone, just in case.

Outside at last in the clean night wind, Jennet and Robin walked toward Tom's house. Robin was silent, but when his hand reached in the darkness to take hers, Jennet exclaimed, "Robin, how could you! You said you'd have nothing to do with her wickedness."

He turned, and although she couldn't make out his look in the darkness, his voice was pleading.

"It's not wickedness, Jennet. I'm not trying to poison anyone or take revenge. It's for you, Jennet."

"No!" She pulled her hand away. "Not for me!"

At Tom's house, Jennet huddled down in a corner, drawing herself away from everything as much as she could. She had no choice but to spend the night here. She wouldn't walk the dark miles back to Kynance alone, not with the sight of the black witch and the swaying devil-beast in her eyes, and no place to shelter at the end of the miles.

Tom was shouting at Robin. The family had gone to bed, all tucked away up in the talfat, but Rob had wakened his brother. They were at the other end of the room, arguing, Tom saying his savings were small enough. But Robin told him what had happened at the witch's house, and at last Tom fell silent. Taking a loose stone from the wall, he dug behind it and handed Robin the coins. Robin went out.

Jennet pulled her shawl over her face and pretended to sleep, as Tom settled down with his family again. The bright morning of this May Day had been like a new beginning. This night she was mired deeper than ever in a muddle of darkness. It was long after Robin returned and lay down by the hearth that Jennet finally slept.

8

The birds were done singing about the sunrise and were well into their day's business when Jennet ran out along the path to Chelew. It was another warm day, though the second of May never had the sparkle of May Day, Jennet reflected. She wondered how An Marget had fared with the feasting and fine clothes. Would the cousins still be there? Or would they be gone—and what state would she find An Marget in? She'd be her strong, calm self, Jennet fervently hoped, else how would she take the news that her apprentice wanted to move in? On the way back from Penmorvah, Jennet had stopped at Robin's cottage to retrieve her bundle. Leave-taking with Rob had been brief and without emotion.

Chelew looked welcoming. The shutters were open, and the cottage stone shone silver-gray in the sunlight.

Beside the house a foam of blossoms was beginning to cover the apple trees, and blooming flowers made bright colors against the old wall below the trees. A small robin flew out a window, a rabbit crouched sunning on the doorstone, and An Marget sat inside, spinning. The wheel hummed, and Marget hummed with it.

She broke off and smiled when she saw Jennet standing in the doorway.

"You're late!" she said. "Hurry in. We have work to do!"

It was as if she'd made a new beginning with the coming of May.

She was not quite so pleased to see Jennet, however, when she heard of Jennet's quarrel with her family.

"Live here?" Marget's brow puckered as she glanced around her neat cottage, and Jennet remembered that the woman was old. "But I—"

Timidly Jennet said, "I could sleep on a blanket in the spence."

The spence was the lean-to room at one end of the house, where supplies were kept.

"I'd be quiet and stay out of your way." She almost whispered with embarrassment.

An Marget shrugged and smiled at her. "All right, child, don't look so homeless. You have a place here."

Jennet could stay at Chelew until the village temper died down, she said. Jan Trevail would get over his anger soon enough, and Molly would miss the pennies Jennet had been bringing home.

Marget directed Jennet to put her bundle in the spence. When Jennet returned, her mistress was still standing in the middle of the room, impatiently waiting for her. The woman's face wasn't old now. It was alight with eagerness, and her eyes flashed.

"Now see what I have!"

An Marget stepped quickly to the oak dresser and took a box from a lower drawer. Placing the box on the table, she produced a small key from her skirt and unlocked the lid. Jennet stood by, wondering what could be inside to excite Marget so. The woman lifted the lid. Inside was a book.

"My cousins brought it," An Marget said. "This, Jennet Trevail, is a copy of *The Key of Solomon*! This belonged to my uncle, the most noted astrologer in the north of Cornwall."

Carefully she lifted the thick book from the box and spread it open for Jennet to see. The pages were of heavy parchment, yellow and brittle with age, and they were covered with handwriting. As An Marget turned the pages, Jennet saw strange words standing out in red ink from the black script, drawings, pages covered with circles and symbols. Some words were underlined, some began with heavy black capital letters. The handwriting was hard to read, but she studied one page until she made out the words "to be invisible."

"*The Key of Solomon* is a conjurer's journal," An Marget's husky voice exulted, "the most famous handbook of magic in existence."

Jennet looked from the script-covered pages to the white witch. Something new was moving in An Marget.

Margaret laughed. "Jennet! Don't look so frightened. This book is full of riches, learning!" She pointed to some words. "What does that say?"

Slowly Jennet puzzled out the handwriting, letter by letter. It had been a long time since she'd seen written words. "The day and hour being ready," she read aloud, "do ye—"

"Good, good!" An Marget nodded in delight. "We will share the search for learning. We'll start at the beginning, and you'll read off the spells to me."

The book was written in the English language. An Marget couldn't read English. Jennet remembered the day An Marget had asked whether she could read, and specifically whether she could read English. The woman must have known her cousins were bringing the book. That's why she'd been so eager for their visit.

And that's why she wanted me—to read, Jennet realized.

That was why the famous Charmer of Kynance had accepted her as an apprentice so easily. Jennet felt like a tool to the old woman's hand.

Yet she remembered that An Marget had instructed her patiently in the use of herbs, sharing her art. She remembered how the white witch's voice had softened after the villagers threatened her. "You don't need to fear the darkness with me, Jennet." Marget had treated her like a trusted apprentice.

And now the white witch was assuming that Jennet would be as eager as she to study the book. She set stools up to the table, one on each side. "Go ahead, read to yourself," she urged. "I'll be ready in a minute."

Clearing the table, she brought paper, an inkstand, a quill pen, and sat down with them at her place. An Marget intended to copy the spells into the Cornish language, Jennet discovered.

Intently the woman looked across the table, her eyes compelling Jennet. When she spoke, the lightness was gone from her voice. "Now, begin."

Handling the pages with care, Jennet turned back to the first one. She glanced up and down the page at the words, studying how the writer made his letters, the peculiar *b*'s and *h*'s. She began to read and translate into Cornish, stumbling, stopping to figure out a word, correcting herself.

" 'A confession to be'—um—'said before thou wake'—no—'worke.' "

Marget's pen scratched slowly on the paper. We're like scholars at work, Jennet thought. She looked up at her mistress, then bent her head over the book again, her hair falling in black curtains at the sides of her face, and read on.

" 'Lord God Almighty Father, Maker of all things, Who knowest all things, for nothing is impossible to Thee—' "

"Why, it's a prayer to God!" Jennet exclaimed.

An Marget smiled. "What did you expect? Instructions for selling our souls to the Devil?"

"Well—"

Resting her pen in the inkstand, An Marget said, "My uncle was a learned man in the science of astrology. One time he came to visit us, and he told me what a great man named Plato once said: The art of magic is the art of worshiping God."

Jennet stared down at the black script, the astrologer's handwriting. Magic, prayers . . . "Is that why you wanted the book? For worshiping God?"

The woman looked at her across the table, and an eyebrow lifted quizzically. "For learning."

Marget picked up her pen and then hesitated as her eyes looked away, unseeing. She murmured, "Perhaps each gain in knowledge means knowing God better."

Jennet shook her head, smiling. It was a mystery— but a mystery unfolding. She gave herself over to the fascination of studying the marvelous book.

" 'Give me grace to know and understand' "—Jennet stopped again. "I don't know the next word."

"That's all right," An Marget said as she dipped the pen and scratched away. "I'll leave spaces for the words you don't know."

Jennet read what she could. "Something—'virtue of all'—something—'by thy most holy'—two words—'by that'—three words—'and fearful name *HVACH*.'" Jennet spelled out the capitals and picked her way through the next few words, ending, "Of all spirits may be opened before me, gently obeying me and my commandments—the most holy *ADONAY*—for ever, amen."

Sometimes the handwriting was difficult to read, but the main trouble was that Jennet knew only the words she'd met in Pastor Thomas' English prayer book. She and An Marget puzzled over the prayer they'd just read. It was asking God for the grace of knowledge, they could tell, but the heart of the prayer was missing. From her prayer book, An Marget thought *Adonay* meant God, but she looked at the book and shook her head over the rest of the words that Jennet pointed out.

Troubled, Marget said, "The words must be said exactly, for the spell to work."

Jennet watched the wisewoman as she closed her eyes and whispered, "Give me grace to know and understand—"

Then the heavy lids lifted, and Margaret's eyes sparkled.

155

"I know! We'll ask Pastor Thomas!"

Jennet smiled in surprise. "What?"

"On a separate paper I'll copy off each word you don't know. You'll take the words to Pastor Thomas to decipher, and you must memorize their meaning. Then we can fill them in." Her face was serene with triumph at her plan.

But Jennet shook her head in dismay. "An Marget, no! He'll never help us with a book of magic. If Pastor Thomas knew—"

"Simply tell him it's a book of medicine, a book of healing," An Marget said calmly. "In a way that's what it is."

Jennet was doubtful. Easy enough for An Marget to say that. She wouldn't be carrying the words to Piggy Thomas. Still, Marget was wiser than she.

Trusting in that, Jennet read on eagerly. All that day and the next she and An Marget studied the ancient script of *The Key of Solomon*. Not a person came to the cottage to disturb them, and they read and wrote day and night, stopping only to eat or to feed the animals or to stroll in the garden to rest their bent shoulders.

Tantalizing fragments of spells and directions appeared: "Here followeth howe the conjurer ought to behave himself." "Here followeth howe experiments for things that are stolen ought to be wrought." "Howe experiments to be invisible must be prepared." The

156

instructions for becoming invisible were very hard to decipher—almost as if on purpose, Jennet thought, amused. In another place she read, "—The day and hour being ready, do ye the experiment appointed you, but first say this prayer following: *Alahac, Falje, Aubonas, Untibolem, Ladodoc—*" The words had a flavor of wild holiness that excited Jennet—like words spoken in a vision.

Jennet didn't know the meaning of the word "experiment" that kept appearing. From her remnants of Latin, An Marget thought it had to do with trying out, but from its place in the sentences, she and Jennet concluded that the word must mean "spell." So for "experiment" An Marget wrote in her manuscript the Cornish word for "spell."

Puzzling over the pages drawn with strange figures, Jennet wondered how their meaning ever could be known without an interpreter. There was a picture of a knife with symbols, words, and crosses drawn along the handle and the blade. On another page was a big circle, with two inner circles. Scattered around the outside of the largest circle were crosses, and inside it were stars. The words on that page read: "How to make the Circle with the Pentacle." Between two stars Jennet spelled out "Tetragrammaton," and in the center, "Master's Circle." It made no sense to Jennet; yet An Marget studied the drawing for a long time, then nodded her head.

Jennet's pleasure in studying the manuscript and in the new companionship with An Marget would have been perfect, except for one thing. She kept worrying about Robin and his plan with An Katty Polteer. In the midst of reading, a word would remind her, and she'd think, *Tomorrow night they will try to raise the dead.* The idea was so unthinkable that her mind flickered away from it.

On the morning of the third day she read out a passage in the book, discovering one word slowly after another.

" 'Lord my God, be Thou to me a Tower of defense against the fear of all evil spirits. Afterwards lett him'—something—'genuflect first to the east, next unto the south, then unto the west and north and in every—' "

A prayer against evil spirits! And the exact directions on how to kneel to make the charm work. This was just the knowledge she'd hoped to learn as a white witch. Yet really—Jennet looked over the words again —it was just a prayer to God. Shouldn't there be more? To banish a spirit, shouldn't there be chants, magical instruments? An Katty Polteer had spoken of rare herbs and ores . . . Return of the dead . . .

Jennet's eyes strayed to look toward the talfat, where Hugh's wedding suit had lain and the boots had moved. Earlier Malachai had flown in the window, and now she saw the magpie perched on the top rung of the ladder, watching her. She looked away from the yellow eyes. An Marget had not mentioned what had happened here on May Day.

Enough of secrecy and darkness, Jennet thought suddenly. There were things she had to know. Yet, for all her current friendliness, the white witch was still awesome. Jennet began cautiously.

"Your cousins visited you, then, on May Day? They brought this book?"

An Marget looked up from her writing and regarded Jennet a moment.

"Yes. They are good people. Once a year they come to me from North Cornwall."

"On your feasten-day?"

There was a longer pause as An Marget looked at Jennet. "My wedding day. Mathy Curnow confessed that he had told you."

Jennet flushed. She felt guilty.

The woman shrugged. "Mathy means well," she said, smiling faintly.

Jennet looked down at the heavy pages, trying to frame her next question, but An Marget said unexpectedly, "And what did you do on May Day?"

The panorama of all she'd done flashed through Jennet's mind.

"I went to Land's End with Robin Pender," she

said hastily and then wished she hadn't. It sounded as though she'd jaunted off like any light-of-fancy country girl.

"Robin Pender."

Jennet could hear the buzzing of a bee in the open window as An Marget's eyes ceased to focus on her and mused inwardly. Then the woman looked back at her.

"Then, Jennet, what are your intentions?"

Jennet lifted her chin. "I am for a white witch."

She looked down at the page. She saw the words "evil spirits" and blurted, "But I dread for Robin!"

Tumbling it out, she told An Marget about the visit to the black witch and what An Katty Polteer proposed to do.

An Marget's eyes narrowed, and she leaned forward. "You must go with them!"

Jennet shrank away. "No!"

Giving a little chuckle, An Marget settled back on her stool and said, "I doubt Katty Polteer could raise a cat, let alone a spirit. But I'd like to know what she does when she tries."

Wouldn't Jennet go along, just for the sake of learning? Marget suggested. Jennet could only shake her head. Surely An Marget understood how it was with her.

"Mistress, I am in terror of spirits," she whispered.

An Marget tapped her pen impatiently. "You'll

have to get over that if you want to be a white witch," she said. "Not all spirits are evil."

Jennet looked around the sunny room for help. Intensely, she said, "An Katty talked of rare herbs and ores. She's going to use magical things to protect against evil when she raises An Sarah's spirit." Then she brought it out. "An Marget, I need to know now. Can you bind and banish a spirit?"

An Marget threw down the pen. Her face was suddenly vivid with emotion, furious. Jennet thought the woman might strike her. But Marget pressed her lips together.

"Someday you will know all that I know," she said. That was all.

Thrusting herself away from the table, the old woman went to her spinning wheel. The wheel whirred angrily for a while, but at last it settled to a hum.

It was late in the morning when she spoke to Jennet again, and then she asked Jennet to carry a request to Robin Pender. After he and An Katty visited the graveyard, would he, of his courtesy, come to Chelew and tell An Marget what had happened? Also, Jennet could carry the first set of words to Pastor Thomas for him to interpret.

Jennet left off dusting the herb pots in the cupboard, where she'd busied herself while An Marget sat silent at the spinning wheel, and folded the sheet of paper into her pocket. She had little liking for either errand, but if she would not go the graveyard—would not!—at least she could obey these requests of her mistress. Her question had not been answered. As she'd worked at the cupboard, Jennet had fluctuated between anger at Marget's evasive reply and dismay that she'd lost Marget's favor.

Voice low, but eyes raised steadily, she told An Marget, "Very well, mistress."

Jennet had not been away from the cottage since she'd moved into Chelew. On her day's errands she had three encounters, and each one was difficult.

First she took the path up into the hills to Robin's farm. She found him near the house, hoeing weeds in a barley field. It was such a homely occupation on a day for raising the dead that Jennet smiled in relief at Rob's strong, bent back. The difficult part came after she told him of An Marget's request, and Rob's lively eyes were intent on her.

"I don't blame you for not coming tonight," he said. "It's stern work for a lass." He grinned. "But if you want to be a witch, you're missing a chance to learn something, sweet Jennet!"

How could he be so light! She almost doubted his good sense.

Robin laughed. "Ah, such a solemn face!" And before she could stop him, he'd hugged her to his chest, and she breathed his warm, earthy smell. "You're mine, Jen, whether you say so or not." He kissed her lightly on the nose.

"Rob." Her voice was a shadow of a sound. She twisted away. "Tonight—take care, Rob. Be safe!" She stared at him and then ran away. She didn't dare picture what would happen in the graveyard. Tears wouldn't be enough.

Next she hurried over the moor and down into Kynance. The village was the same as she'd left it before May Day, barren and gray in the spring greenness of the valley. The mud had dried in the lanes, but the clay huts and granite cottages squatted as gloomily as ever in the sunlight, with no sprig of greenery to soften them. A few women stood gossiping in their dooryards. As Jennet passed, they turned away from her, and one woman hastily pulled her child behind her skirts. Uneasily Jennet realized that no one had come to the white witch for help since the night she'd cursed Gracey Winkey.

Jennet wanted to speak to someone in the village. She wanted news of her family, and she'd like to send word to Nancy that she was living with An Marget. Then if Nan walked out to Chelew one day, Jennet could find out how Jan Trevail had taken her leaving.

A woman emerged from a shed, carrying a pail of milk. Jennet knew her slightly, as she knew everyone in the village.

"Mistress Trella, can you tell me—" As she hurried over to the dooryard, she saw that the woman had a rag tied around the hand not carrying the bucket. "Oh," she said involuntarily, "you've hurt yourself."

The woman tried to pass. "I'm in a hurry," she muttered.

Jennet looked at the bandaged hand, not moving out of the way. The rag was dirty, and red puffiness showed around its edges. As she looked, Jennet's hand began to feel hot. It throbbed with fever, just as Mistress Trella's hand must be throbbing. Jennet was frightened. It had happened unexpectedly as always, for no reason, feeling someone else's pain. Yet if her hand really were ailing like the woman's, she knew just the herb poultice she'd make to take out the sickness.

"I can heal your hand," she told the woman eagerly. "Come to Chelew, and I'll make—"

"No!" The woman turned quickly, slopping out some milk. "Please, leave me alone!" She ran back to the shed.

She's afraid of me, Jennet thought. Slowly she walked on, and the fever in her hand faded away, but she felt a sickness of dismay.

Then she came to the church, and she forgot Mistress Trella. She had to go through the graveyard to reach Pastor Thomas' house in the back, beyond the hedge. Jennet climbed the stone steps up the slight bank, noticing some clouds in the blue sky. The church tower rose beside her like a cliff, the yew tree stood tall and black against the sky—but she couldn't keep looking upward. In spite of herself, her eyes looked down. There was the mound that covered Sarah Pender's body. Jennet stood in the grassy yard, where gravestones grew instead of flowers. A hedge and the stone of the church enclosed the place from the village, and though she heard the faint chatter of children in the lanes, the graveyard held its own silence. Glancing, she saw that grass and ivy had begun to creep across the mound. Robin and An Katty would come here tonight — Jennet ran to the gate in the hedge that led into Pastor Thomas' yard.

The priest's house was built like the others in Kynance, but as Jennet knocked on the door, she noticed something different about the windows on either side of it. The windows were filled in with glass, not simply shuttered over. How fine for Piggy Thomas! She studied the panes set into diamonds of lead and remembered she'd seen windows like these in St. Ives. No one came to the door. Then Jennet heard voices beyond the house. Going around to the back, she noted little fruit trees, covered with blossom, growing in a sheltered corner of a walled garden, and there were grapevines against the wall. She found the round little pastor fussing at a village boy who was weeding a vegetable plot.

"No, no, don't pull that up! *Those* are the peas

coming up, *those* are the weeds!" He thrust a stick at the plants, pointing, then whacked the boy on the shoulders for good measure. "Use what brains you've got!"

Jennet felt sorry for the boy. Pastor Thomas chose his house and garden help from the village folk in place of a tithe from those families, and the boy would get no pay for the hard knocks.

Pastor Thomas noticed Jennet standing there.

"What's the matter?" he said anxiously. "Is someone dead?"

Jennet smiled. Kynance people called on their priest only when they needed his official services—for christenings, weddings, and funerals.

She bobbed a curtsy. "No, sir. It's a matter of healing," she said, choosing her words carefully. "You know, sir, that I work for An Marget, who makes medicine for the sick?"

The boy's head came up to listen, and Pastor Thomas noticed him. "Tend to your business, boy," he said. He trotted to the bench under the pear trees at the other end of the garden, motioning Jennet to follow him. He sat, but Jennet stood politely before him. "Now," he said with a nasal sound, looking up at her. She was aware of the two round nostrils in his short nose, just like a pig's snout.

"An Marget has a book of healing."

She told him that she was reading the book to her

mistress because it was written in English, saying tactfully, "I can still read, thanks to your teaching, sir." Then, explaining that there were some words that she didn't understand, she begged his learned help and produced the paper from her pocket.

Pastor Thomas took the paper, held it out to study it, brought it close, pursed his lips. "Yes, yes," he nodded. "Healing. Old Marget is a good woman for relieving little aches and pains," he murmured, squinting at the words, "as there is no physician here."

He looked up at Jennet and raised his finger. "But one must always remember that real calamities may be the will of God," he instructed her. "Punishments. The people should not try to avoid their just punishments."

Jennet had heard the same thing said from the pulpit. "But, sir," she ventured, "our Lord Jesus Christ healed lepers, terrible ailments."

Pastor Thomas smiled. "I hope An Marget doesn't think she's Christ." He chuckled and shook his head. "Heal like Christ, ha ha."

Jennet waited. Pastor Thomas returned to the paper and began reading off the words.

" 'Unceasing.' That means without stopping. 'Summoning'—calling to a place. Um—ummm—'inef—' " He held the paper at arm's length. "Inef-fa-ble." He mouthed the syllables. "That means—um—well, it doesn't matter. It's just a kind of connecting word, you know."

Jennet nodded doubtfully, trying to see the sheet and memorize the meanings. The pastor glanced down the list, murmuring words as Jennet listened and noted them. Then—

"'Penta'— What's this? 'Pentacle!' I've heard of that. It's a kind of magician's star. Jennet Trevail!" He looked up at her in horror. "Has An Marget got a book of magic? I won't have any witchcraft in my parish!"

Despite Jennet's dismay, she almost laughed as she thought suddenly of An Katty's plans for Piggy Thomas' graveyard tonight.

"I want to see that book," he was saying. "Bring it to me."

"Well—the book is very old and fragile, sir," Jennet said, trying to put him off. "I don't think An Marget would let me carry it about. Perhaps if you came to Chelew—" Pastor Thomas never stirred out to visit the cottages.

"No!" He hitched his round bottom on the bench. "I'm too busy."

"But—the rest of the words—"

Pastor Thomas cried, "Nay! I'll have nothing to do with An Marget!"

Jennet saw that his face was full of fear.

"Here!" He thrust the paper at her as if it would burn him. "Take this away!"

And then, as Jennet walked away, he called after

her, his voice almost pleading, "But tell Marget I tried to help, there's a good girl."

Why, he was afraid of An Marget. Where was his pastor's trust in a good God, Jennet thought scornfully, if he feared a white witch? She hurried out of the garden. No wonder Kynance people found a hollow church. Piggy Thomas never preached about the goodness of God, only about how God would punish the people if they didn't obey Him. As she ran past the gravestones and came by the church door, she thought, It was our church long before *he* came. She looked back and saw his fat face watching her over the hedge. Defiantly, she turned into the church porch and went inside.

Opposite the mermaid pew she knelt. Never mind Piggy Thomas. *Lord God*, she prayed, *take care of Robin Pender tonight. Don't let any spirits come back from the dead.* It was such a hasty, awkward prayer. *Our Father Who art in heaven*—she said the familiar words—*temptation, deliver us from evil*—

She looked up at the window over the altar, where the Christ hung on the Cross, between the sun and the moon, colors glowing from the sunlight outside. She studied the features of the face, trying to see His goodness as a healer, but it was a sad, remote face. Straight nose, large eyes slightly tilted . . . Her eyes wandered, and she saw the pisky face laughing in the wooden screen. Straight nose, slanted eyes . . . *Tch*, she clicked her tongue and smiled in amazement. The features, the face—they were the same person. That was how Christ would look if He were laughing.

9

That night at Chelew when supper was over, Jennet looked around for something to do so that she wouldn't think about what was going on in the graveyard. The shutters were drawn against the damp night air, a furze fire crackled in the fireplace, An Marget sat with her knitting—truly, Chelew was a cozy, sheltered place. A rabbit dozed by the fire, and Jennet sprawled her skirts on the hearthstone to play with the furry creature. She teased a straw over the rabbit's drooping ears, until it woke and nuzzled its soft nose at her hand for something to eat. But when she'd found some chunks of meal and fed them to the rabbit, it went back to sleep in her lap. She stroked the downy fur, half-noticing its feel between her fingers as she watched the blue and yellow flames of the fire, leaping, curling, changing as the furze burned and settled.

She should have gone with Robin. If she loved him—yet how could she have helped him, fearful as she was? Only God—*God, if you're good, keep him safe.*

A twig of furze caught fire and glowed and writhed like a red snake. It would be a long time to wait until Robin came to tell what had happened—of course he would come. The sands in the hourglass would have to go down many times. No doubt the black witch would work her spell at midnight. Jennet wondered how An Katty Polteer would get to Robin's house and then to Kynance. She pictured the old woman hurrying over the dark moor with her sideways hobble. It would be a long walk. Would Robin carry her? Jennet saw the witch mounted on Robin's back like a demon and shuddered. The rabbit woke and hopped away from her lap.

An Marget looked up from her knitting. "Let's occupy our minds for a while, Jennet."

They should fill in the words Pastor Thomas had explained, she said, while Jennet's memory was fresh. Marget took the conjurer's manuscript from its box in the oak cupboard and placed it on the table, along with her copying sheets and the inkstand. Jennet would rather not have thought about magic at all on this night, but she took the list of words from her pocket and sat down beside An Marget. They bent their heads over the manuscripts, *The Key of Solomon* and Marget's Cornish translation, hunting the places for the missing words.

" 'Unceasing,' " Jennet began, "see in that prayer, there—it means without stopping," she spoke it in Cornish. " 'Particle' means *didjan*."

The work went slowly, finding the words on Jennet's list in the ancient script and fitting them to the blanks in Marget's manuscript. "Kerchief" was *nacken* in Cornish. "Lichen" meant *kewny*, "frog" meant *quilkan*, "toad" meant *cronack*.

Jennet watched Marget's scratching pen. She wanted nothing to do with brews made of toads. That smacked of black magic—not white magic, she thought, wondering again about the book. An Marget looked up for the next word.

A "pentacle" was a kind of magician's star, Jennet explained. That was all Pastor Thomas had translated. She'd already told Marget what had happened in the interview, and the old woman had shrugged and murmured something about enough fat between the ears to boil cabbage. Now An Marget studied again the diagram in the book, where the words explained "How to make the circle with the Pentacle."

"What does it mean?" Jennet asked suddenly. "You seem to know what the circle is for, how it's used."

"Yes." Marget glanced at her, hesitating, then said matter-of-factly, "It's a circle of protection for the person who is calling up a spirit. Let's hope old Katty knows how to make a circle tonight." She chuckled.

Jennet drew back, her mouth grimacing. "But that's black witchcraft!"

The woman lifted her eyebrows. She rose and put away the papers and the book and sat down by the fire to knit. Jennet watched her sitting there, powerful charmer, but good woman. An Marget wouldn't use the things of black witchcraft. Of course, if the circle were used for good . . . Robin would say calling up An Sarah's spirit was for good . . . but An Katty was a black witch. Surely there must be a line between good and evil. No, she wouldn't think about it.

Jennet sat near the fire, and its warmth felt good. It was a low, comforting fire. The hour must be late. There was nothing to do. When she'd flung together her bundle, she hadn't thought to bring along her knitting of stockings, as the old woman was doing. Usually if folk sat up this late, it was to tell tales around the fire. Jennet wished An Marget would chat with stories of her girlhood. She glanced at the woman, who sat remote and silent, the clicking of her needles the only sound.

"Did you ever study with your uncle, the astrologer?" Jennet asked.

"No, I saw him only the one time," Marget said. The needles clicked. "I wish I could have, for he knew how to calculate cures by the junctures of the planets."

174

She laughed. "And how to plot the evil moment for ill-wishing to take effect. Oh, Mathy!" She shook her head, smiling, and lapsed into silence again.

Astrologer . . . juncture of planets . . . The words echoed and faded. Jennet stared into the glowing chunks of furze, and her mind drifted, warm and easy, not thinking. Shapes of moods shifted and blended, like slow clouds moving across the sky.

And then she heard Robin laughing. Not with her ears, not by imagining how his laughter sounded, but as if her mind was receiving the sound. Somewhere Robin was laughing in great surprised guffaws.

"Robin's all right!" she exclaimed. "He's laughing. I can hear him!"

An Marget glanced toward the doorway.

"No, not outside—but somewhere. I hear him." She touched the side of her forehead.

An Marget gazed down at Jennet on the hearth, her eyes softened by the shadows. "Young Jennet," she mused, "I wish I had your gifts." Her voice was like the furry down of the rabbit.

Gifts? Yes, it was a good thing to know that Robin was laughing, and surely a demon couldn't make goodness.

They waited while the fire simmered and the needles clicked, and before long they both heard male laughter outside. There was pounding on the door and a shout, "Hello in there!"

An Marget rose with some dignity and went without hurry to answer the brash knocking. It was Robin who stood outside, and he began, "Ho, there, Marget!" But then he calmed to a more proper respect at the sight of her. Jennet noted the regal tilt of An Marget's head, and she was amused when Robin's face fell in sheepish-boy lines and he said meekly, "May I come in, Mistress Margaret?" She suspected he'd never seen the Charmer of Kynance, and she was still indignant over his allegiance to Witch Katty.

Nevertheless, Jennet was so happy to see Robin that of a sudden she glowed with the warmth of the fire. This midnight cottage was the best place in the world, with Robin Pender in it. She pulled her bare feet under her skirts and smiled at him.

An Marget took her seat in the oak chair, pointing Robin to the bench she'd vacated.

"And how is An Sarah Pender?" she asked. The corner of her mouth twitched.

Robin grinned at her in return and said frankly, "Mistress Margaret, I suppose I'll never know, unless you could tell me."

Jennet leaned forward, clasping her knees. "What happened? Tell!"

"Well then," he began, "An Katty should act in a mummer's play. If she isn't a witch, she knows how to play the role!"

Long after dark, when he was wrought up with

waiting, the old woman had come scratching at his door, not knocking like an honest person. She carried a forked stick, and he got the startled impression she'd ridden over from Penmorvah on it. However, she condescended to scramble along beside him as they set off down the hills toward Kynance Churchyard.

First off she'd demanded, did he have the courage to do this? Was he sure he could face his aunt's spirit with a clean conscience? She soon had him prickling with nerves, Robin said, as she wheezed about the other and evil spirits that might appear along with An Sarah's. She kept telling him he must be brave and not fear, for she had in her pouch pocket the rare herbs to throw at the demons. Then as they'd walked through the lanes of the village she began to moan strange words, some kind of spell, and he had to keep his hands in his pockets, they were so cold.

"There's a fog out, too," Robin muttered, "in case you didn't know. The wispy kind that keeps shifting."

As they'd neared the Church Cross square there was a pounding of feet behind them, but he could see nothing. It was the Devil's hounds hurrying to the place, An Katty told him. But he shouldn't fear, once they were on consecrated ground, for the demons couldn't enter. Only the spirits of the dead had a right to the hallowed place.

Suddenly she had let out a shriek. She saw one now! See—she'd clutched Rob's arm—see there, perching on the church tower! Ah, now she saw the ghosts glimmering all over the roof, and there went one flitting to the top of the yew tree. Couldn't Robin see them?

He couldn't tell what he saw, the way the mist drifted around the church and the tree. He sweated cold drops, and he wanted to run.

"No!" he'd said loudly. "I don't see spirits!"

Then An Katty had been, oh, so kind. In her wheedling voice she'd offered to rub his eyes with the salve from the corners of her eyes, so he could see the wondersome ghosts too. He'd shied away from her, gripping the solid stone column of the Church Cross. The black witch coaxed him to enter into the graveyard. Ghosts were nothing to fear, she said, just poor shadows of their worn-out bodies. See the light in the church window? They liked to go in there and act over their weddings and funerals, especially their funerals, her voice had whispered, burying one another over and over in every style folks dead or alive could imagine. But he must come along. She could feel An Sarah's spirit, impatient to come out of the grave. No witch had released her yet.

He thought of Jennet, Robin said, and what he wanted for her. He told himself he was a man. He set each foot down firmly, to stop the trembling of his legs. Following the old crone, he entered the graveyard.

The stones stood up in the mist, and the silence was so heavy he could almost hear the settling of drifts of fog. As they approached the mound that was An Sarah's grave, all covered with the whiteness of mist, the witch moaned that despite the consecrated ground she felt evil around her. It was powerful tonight. Did he want to go back? Maybe they should come another time. Robin said No. Then An Katty began to chant weird words and throw foul-smelling stuff into the fog.

An Marget leaned forward. "What did she say?"

Robin waved for her to wait and went on. Next, An Katty had taken her forked stick and drawn a circle on the grass around her and Robin where they stood near the grave. The charmed circle would protect them, she said. She began an incantation, her voice quavering into the mist of the graveyard, slowly pronouncing long, strange words. Holding her stick out toward the mound, she called in a louder voice:

"Spirit of Sarah Pender, in the name of all the powers above and below, I summon thee to arise from thy grave! By the spirits of fire, air, earth, and water, I summon thee to arise. Come hither, appear and speak to this man!"

This she said three times, her voice louder each time until it ended in a shriek.

There was silence. Robin said he'd stood trembling in the silence. Then suddenly unearthly howls and shrieks seemed to come out of the grave. Slowly, from the fog heavy over the mound, something white rose and wavered, wraithlike.

"Behold, the spirit!" the witch screeched.

Terrified, Robin cried out, "In the name of God, who or what are you?"

He could see no face or arms, only the whiteness of a shape.

The specter spoke in a hollow voice. "I, Sarah, come from the grave to tell thee where I hid the money." The low voice stopped, then continued, "But when you find it, you must give half of all that is mine to this powerful woman, Katty Polteer. If you don't, I'll come back and haunt you—Devil take me, if I don't!" The voice twanged out the last words and hiccoughed.

Robin said he thought he'd heard that voice before, and upon hearing the familiar phrase, he jumped forward. His nose met a strong smell of whiskey. Tugging at the white shape, he jerked off a cloth, and there stood a man jabbering at him.

"It was nobody but that old lutterpooch, Tammy Polteer!" Robin exclaimed. He let out a shout of laughter at the look on Jennet's face.

It was all up with An Katty then. She ran scrambling away, dropping her stick. Robin couldn't beat a woman, so he'd snatched up the stick and whacked Tammy a couple of good ones across the shoulders. The last Robin saw of his "ghost" was Tammy shuffling off in the fog to find his old woman.

"So I'm out five shillings," Rob said ruefully, "and I still don't know where the will is. Or my savings." He looked at Jennet. "I'm a fool."

"Ah, no," she began; then An Marget snorted.

Marget flung a hand over her mouth, but a chuckle came out anyway, and then an explosion of laughter. "Ha—oh, ha ha! Oh, Robin, forgive me!" She shook with laughter. "That silly old woman and her drunken ghost!"

Rob laughed with her readily. "It's all right; I've been laughing all the way down here. 'Devil take me, if I don't,' " he mimicked and guffawed.

Jennet could just picture that old timnoodle playing ghost, and suddenly it tickled her. "Ha ha ha!" she pealed out. No spirit sucking Robin into a grave—only a hiccoughing ghost! She laughed until her eyes were wet.

"And there weren't any ghosts on the church roof?" she stopped to ask seriously. She'd sat breathless with the tale from that point on.

Rob shook his head, grinning at her. "No ghosts, love, no demons."

Nothing but foolishness. She'd prayed, she'd trusted God—and Robin was safe.

"I heard you laughing," Jennet said happily, "long before you came."

If all her visions could be such good ones—

Curious, Robin asked how she could have heard him, but Jennet couldn't explain, though An Marget said Jennet had indeed mentioned the experience. Robin studied Jennet warily. Until now, he'd had a way of looking at her intimately that excited her. Now his look became tinged with respect, and oddly, Jennet felt rather lonely.

An Marget was speaking thoughtfully. "Probably you'll find the will and the savings someday, tucked away in the thatch or behind a stone in the wall. But it's possible someone has stolen them."

"Well then—" Rob shrugged. How would they ever know?

Jennet saw that An Marget had something in mind. "Listen," she counseled.

Marget questioned—his brother knew about the expedition with An Katty? Others? Rob nodded sheepishly. Then let them believe he had seen An Sarah's ghost, An Marget suggested. Robin should not explain in detail, simply let it be thought that Sarah Pender's specter had spoken to him in the graveyard. The news would spread fast enough.

Jennet giggled suddenly. What a tricky one An Marget was!

Robin watched the woman's expressionless face, puzzled. "Do you mean—"

"If there is a thief, you'll put the fear of a ghost into him!" Marget said. "One fine morning you might find the will and the savings in a tidy bundle on your doorstep."

Robin laughed. "Mistress Margaret, you are a wise woman! It's good to find sense in a witch, instead of dark hocus-pocus."

Marget received his praise serenely and bent her head to her knitting again.

Rob tugged his ear. "But won't An Katty tell what happened?"

"Not she!" Jennet said.

Robin saw it at once. "No, of course not."

"You might even get your five shillings back," Marget murmured over her knitting wool. "Threaten *you'll* tell if she doesn't return the money. Old Katty won't like being exposed as a joke." She smiled at her knitting. "Though I'd love to see that happen."

The plans were settled then, and Robin had back his confidence when he rose to leave. Jennet was pleased with his new respect for her mistress, but the cottage was not as warm when he'd gone. Sternly, she told herself to forget these yearnings. She and Robin would be seeing each other in passing in the village for the rest of their lives, and this intimacy must cease. Maybe, she thought wistfully, when she was an old and respected white witch, Robin would be a friend to her as Uncle Mathy was to An Marget. It was not a very exciting thought.

10

No one came to Chelew. The days of May passed, warm and sweet with the smell of gorse at noon, chill and misty at night. Sudden thunderstorms swept in from the sea and passed. And no one came to An Marget for advice or herbs or charms.

One evening Jennet saw An Marget walking slowly along the path toward Kynance, and Jennet followed her. The woman stopped beyond the curve of hill and looked down toward the gray village in its green valley. Jennet stood beside her in silence, then spoke for Marget.

"No one comes."

"Fools," An Marget said, but her voice was uncertain.

In the days that went by, her attention was all for the book of magic, and her concentration began to make Jennet uneasy. Morning after morning An Marget made Jennet read to her while she copied the translation on her papers. When Jennet came to an unfamiliar word, An Marget told her impatiently to skip over it; they'd find someone to explain it later. She seemed in a feverish search for something in particular in the book.

Often Malachai presided over the study. Jennet would glance up at the magpie and think what a scene they presented—on a dark rainy day, woman and girl with heads bent over the ancient manuscript, one candle lit on the table beside them, black bird brooding on its perch on top of the cabinet. Occasionally Malachai burst into a chatter of squawking bird sounds, but he seldom spoke words, to Jennet's relief. Though once in the midst of the reading aloud he said suddenly "Heigh-ho," and he sounded so bored that Jennet almost laughed.

Another time An Marget looked up at the magpie and said abruptly, "Who cries?"

"Fools cry," replied Malachai in that hollow voice. "Fools cry."

Jennet had never seen the white witch use Malachai in her acts of brewing herbs or saying charms. Perhaps the magpie was not a familiar or a demon, but simply, as Marget first said, a bird she'd taught to talk. Something to talk to in solitary times. Yet if that were true—Jennet thought of the words Marget had chosen to teach him: "I will come," "Go away," "Only the wicked," "Fools cry," and the one light word, "Heigh-ho."

As the reading of prayers and directions for magic went on, Jennet began to lose her fascination with the book. She had growing suspicions that were confirmed when she read off, "Howe experiments for hatred are prepared that any may be made enemies." Despite the prayers to God, this conjurer's work was not all for good. She stopped. Preparing hatred wasn't worshiping God. But An Marget pressed her on.

The woman's tension quivered along Jennet's nerves, and when she could, she escaped to the sunny garden to work among the plants. Now she sang only over the sage plants growing among the marjoram. An Marget had suggested that, to see if singing really did help the plants to grow, and it did seem that the new clump flourished more than the bits of sage left in their old spot. Singing, Jennet laughed a little at herself, but she was serious in her affection for the sage she'd transplanted.

One morning An Marget asked Jennet to take grain to the mill to be ground. When Jennet went to the spence, she discovered that the barley bin was nearly empty. The old woman had no fields and depended on the sacks of grain left on her doorstone by grateful villagers. No gifts had appeared on the stone for a long time now. As she filled a sack, Jennet thought guiltily of the food she consumed at An Marget's table. She wondered if there were any gold coins left from the hoard An Marget was said to have brought to Kynance. Probably not, after thirty years. Of course, when a saddler came riding out the coast from St. Ives, Marget sold him the good thread she spun. But to spin, she needed flax, and no flax had come to the door either.

Jennet set off for the mill, pondering on how she might mend matters. If she could show she was harmless . . . Waiting by the millpond was the usual cluster of women and children, as well as Gracey Winkey and Dolly the Duck, who seemed to walk up to the mill almost every morning to gossip.

"Good day, Mistress Pendower," Jennet said pleasantly to the innkeeper's wife.

The woman nodded and moved toward the door of the mill. The others glanced at Jennet and carefully looked away. Even Gracey kept her silence. Today there were no taunts. Instead, the women were quietly wary.

Jennet sat down on the wall and tried again. To Dolly she said, "Wasn't that a fine bonfire on May Day Eve?"

"Aye," the fat woman said. "I saw you dancing." Her eyes speculated on Jennet, and Jennet felt her face flush.

Then there was more silence, the women's eyes trying to find someplace to look. No one would speak for fear of saying the wrong thing, Jennet realized. At last they began to talk trivia to one another in hushed tones, but she saw she'd cast a pall on the morning's gathering. She was glad when someone motioned her ahead to take an early turn, and she could escape from the oppressive atmosphere. Time, she told herself. After a time they'd get over their fears. An Marget had been respected in Kynance too long for the people to forsake her forever.

On the way back through the village, she stepped into the church. She wanted to look again at the faces of the Christ and the pisky, to see whether she'd fancied it or they really were the same. Automatically she knelt in a pew and then looked up through the dusky sea light. The Christ face was immediate, lit on color by light through the stained glass, but she had to hunt the pisky face among the shadowed wood carvings. The resemblance was still there, one face awesome, the other laughing. God laughing. Jennet remembered how good it had felt when they'd all laughed at An Katty's imaginary ghosts.

But what about real demons? Would God laugh at those? Surely evil was a serious matter, and He would put on His awesome face. Yet—Jennet shifted uneasily on her knees as she stared back and forth at the two faces—wasn't that something like defeat? Surely, too, God's laughter couldn't be defeated by evil. Maybe His laughter was so strong with goodness that He'd laugh despite the Devil's attempts.

But she couldn't. Jennet tried to picture herself laughing away evil spirits as they wove like smoke in a room, and she felt only fear. It was impossible. She bowed her head against the next pew in despair.

When she went out of the church, the sack of barley flour was a heavy drag on her hand. However, beyond the village Jennet cheered a little when she spied two men coming up from the cove. They were Uncle Mathy Curnow and Jack Tregear, and they were pulling a sledge heaped with seaweed and sand.

"Ho, Jennet!" Captain Mathy called.

Jennet left the path and ran down to meet the men. They eased the ropes from their shoulders.

"Demned heavy work!" Uncle Mathy puffed. His face was redder than ever, but his eyes twinkled with good spirits.

"Tell that Margaret woman I'm doing as she says," he ordered, "bringing up dressing for my fields. Those poor ill-wished cattle sorely need better grass."

"Aye," Tregear said, winking at Jennet. "He's nursing them, now they've been so ill-wished."

"None of your lip," Mathy growled, "or I'll put you to mending my hedges too."

Jennet smiled at him. She thought now that the bottle of water had no magic at all, but only carried An

Marget's power to make people believe in it. And Mathy had believed in it, too—or had chosen to.

"Come visit An Marget," she told the old man, "and bring your tales. We're lonely at Chelew."

Uncle Mathy looked guilty and rubbed his beard. Jennet suspected he knew very well how the people were treating Marget since the cursing.

"That I will," he said. "Just as soon as this mort of field work is done, that I will, and gladly."

Jack Tregear made a joke about the work, and they all parted, laughing.

The next Sunday Jennet went to church. When An Marget saw her putting on her good dress, she asked why Jennet bothered to go to hear Piggy Thomas oink.

"Well, he's not the only one there," Jennet retorted and then was embarrassed. An Marget would think she was looking for Robin, and that wasn't why she wanted to go.

She went late on purpose, to avoid the before-service gatherings under the Courtyard Cross. Slipping into the last pew, she saw the Trevail family farther forward and Rob's head shining faintly in the light from a slit window on the side. The service had begun. As she followed it, she saw Pastor Thomas look down the length of the church and eye her disapprovingly. Defiantly she spoke out the words of the psalm as loudly as the rest. She was part of this community, and she had a right to worship in this church. Ignoring Piggy Thomas, she concentrated on the deep eyes of the Christ face and the twinkling eyes in the pisky face. Sometimes she looked at the back of Jan Trevail's rough-combed head.

Service over, Jennet was one of the first out and tried to hurry away unnoticed. But Robin pushed between the people, and before she could leave the churchyard, he caught her arm.

"Ho, Miss Witch! I have news for you."

She whirled to look up at his happy face. "You've found the money!"

"No." He shrugged ruefully. "Not yet. But other money is appearing."

"Appearing?" For a foolish moment Jennet pictured gold coins appearing out of the air. "What do you mean?"

Robin drew her aside from the people coming away from the church and spoke in a low voice. "Of course the story got around that I'd gone to the graveyard. Mary, my sister-in-law, had to waggle her tongue. So!" He grinned. "When people ask me whether I saw Sarah Pender's ghost, I say, 'It was a fearful night, but An Sarah is going to help me.'"

He imitated the foreboding voice he used, and Jennet giggled.

"Now, Mistress Jennet, what do you think?" Rob

went on. "Not only do people believe I saw a ghost, but they're beginning to say they've seen An Sarah, too. Dolly the Duck reports she saw her in a black shawl, walking in the lanes at dusk. Someone else saw her specter going over a hill." He chuckled. "And the folk have it all figured out. They say An Sarah Pender won't rest until justice is done."

Jennet shook her head in amazement. Staying so close with Marget at Chelew, she hadn't heard a word of this.

"But—the money?" she asked.

Robin laughed. "Why, don't you see? They're all afraid she'll haunt them, for she was crabbed enough in life. Everyone who ever borrowed an egg from her, everyone who owed her even a penny, everyone who said an ill word about An Sarah is secretly leaving payment on my doorstep. Coins, settings of eggs, sacks of grain, even butter!" Robin gestured in delight.

Jennet saw Anne Pendower smiling hesitantly at her and smiled in return. She noticed other people watching her and Robin. The usual after-church visiting was going on in the graveyard. In the rainy winter, people left soon, their heads drooping in dark, hooded clusters. But now in the bright May, their hoods and hats came off, and they lifted their heads to the sun like flowers. Jennet saw Uncle Mathy laughing with some men, so the village grudge toward him must have worn off. Yet laughter stopped when people glanced toward

Robin and Jennet. Jennet wondered, would they come to fear lighthearted Rob-Bob, too? He shouldn't be seen with her.

"I'm glad for your good fortune," she said. She moved to leave, but Robin followed her.

"That's not all."

Everyone in the Pender clan was willing for him to keep the gifts and work the farm, he said, for fear An Sarah would begrudge them. None had any better claim to the farm than he, and each was afraid to press a claim, in case Robin had really been named heir in the will.

"Tell An Marget she's a wise woman, and I'll come with my thanks and sharing of the gifts!"

As for An Katty Polteer—Rob began laughing again—she'd been so afraid he'd expose her that she'd handed back Tom's five shillings when Robin had visited her. Old Tammy hadn't taken them to St. Ives at all.

"So all's well!" he concluded. "Or nearly all."

They had reached the courtyard below the church. Robin took Jennet by the shoulders and squared her around to look down at her, his face serious now.

"Jennet, An Katty's ghosts were only imaginary. Why can't you forget your fears and come to me?"

She looked down, not to see Robin's face. From the sides of her eyes she saw the feet of people walking by.

"Some demons are real," she said in a low voice.

He lifted her chin so that she had to look at him. His green eyes were intense.

"Forget me!" she whispered. "I won't have you!"

He smiled. "But you will," he said, releasing her. "One day you'll come to me, Jennet."

Robin looked lighthearted and was laughing again as she ran away, and Jennet marveled at how he could keep trusting in spite of the facts. He's a fool, too, she told herself indignantly. And cruel. Couldn't he see how he was tormenting her?

Monday, the sun was gone in a chill drizzle, and it was a long gray day inside Chelew. Weary of straining her eyes over the foreign handwriting in the book, Jennet was preparing to go to bed on her quilts in the spence when someone knocked on the door. She hurried into the big room in time to see An Marget admitting a hooded woman carrying a bundle, light rain gusting through the doorway after her. The woman threw back the hood of her cloak, and it was Nancy who stood there. It was Jemmy she carried, bundled in a blanket.

"An Marget, Jennet, you must help!" Nancy cried. "It's the kinkcough!"

Jemmy squirmed out of her arms as he gasped and struggled for breath. Bending over, the little boy broke into a sharp, ringing cough. Jennet sprang to him. A child could die of exhaustion from the dreaded whooping cough.

"Red clover," An Marget said, already moving to the herb cupboard. "Help him, Jennet, while I prepare the medicine."

How could she help him? Sitting in the tall chair, she tried to make Jemmy comfortable on her lap, holding him up as he gasped for air. Nancy sat on the bench opposite, barely resting on the edge in her agitation. Her usually placid face was so distraught she hardly looked like herself.

"How long has this been going on?" Jennet asked. Jemmy had seemed all right in church yesterday.

"Just tonight." Nancy clasped her hands. "Oh, Jen, it was awful. He'd gone to bed early, and all of a sudden he burst into a fit of coughing, but we didn't think much of it, and nobody went to him. Then Dick called down from the talfat that Jemmy was dying! Oh, Jen, he was all blue in the face from trying to get a breath! We thumped his back until he got air, but all he can do is wheeze. Molly was afraid for me to bring him to you, but she didn't know what else to do."

Jemmy flailed his hands as he sucked in a squeaking breath, and Jennet bent her head to him, whispering, soothing.

Nancy chattered on. "At home they didn't know whether you and Marget are for good or evil, but I say for good. Anyway, I knew you wouldn't work harm on your brother."

Jennet could see An Marget mixing the dried clover flowers into a kettle of water over the fire, adding honey. How could Nancy even suspect evil was brewing? She looked at her sister sadly and spoke, her breath coming with difficulty.

"It may not be the kinkcough, if he hasn't"—she wheezed—"been sick before. You know how children usually have a cold first." Jennet gasped between words, and Jemmy squirmed in her arms as he gave barking coughs. "Maybe—it's a croupy cough."

She was choking for air. "Jemmy—where does it feel the worst?"

"Here," he said hoarsely. He put his hand on his throat and upper chest. "Jennet, make it—all right," he begged.

She nodded and hugged him so he wouldn't be frightened to see how she, too, was struggling to breathe. She was suffering with him, her throat full, as if stuffed with wool. Jennet felt her eyes bulging as she strained for a breath and saw Nancy staring at her. If only she could breathe some of the rainy air into her thick throat—no, not cold night air, warm air.

Jennet jumped up with Jemmy and ran to the hearth, where An Marget had just swung the steaming kettle off the fire.

"Not to drink—breathe!" she choked.

Hooking an edge of the blanket to a peg on the fireplace wall, she flung the blanket over herself and the child, enclosing them with the hanging kettle. She knelt under the blanket with it draped against her back and stood Jemmy on the floor.

"Keep trying to breathe," she ordered. "Breathe the good air."

Obediently, he sucked and wheezed. Soon the sweet-smelling steam was thick under the heavy wool blanket, and Jennet thought of clover fields basking in warm sunlight. She pulled the steam into her throat and presently, as it penetrated, the scent of clover and honey was stronger. The blanket grew damp and warm, open on one side to the flaming furze in the fireplace. Jennet kept her hands on Jemmy's chest, and she felt him relax, not struggling so hard to breathe.

"Good steam," she whispered to him through her thick throat, "breathe the sweet steam. In—out, in—out," she said in slow rhythm.

"Jen, it's getting better," he murmured sleepily.

There was silence from beyond the blanket. She didn't know what An Marget and Nancy were doing, or what her mistress thought of her taking command of the cough potion. Now air went down her throat easily, the congestion gone, the honeyed damp air like a sweet bath to her nose and throat. Jemmy nestled against her and went to sleep. She smoothed his wet forehead and bent her head close to his face. His breathing was gentle. At last, Jennet tucked him up in the bottom folds of the blanket and crawled out of the shelter.

An Marget was sitting in the tall chair now, quietly knitting, and Nancy sat on the settle, watching, her face smooth again.

"How is he?" Marget asked, and when Jennet nodded and smiled, she raised an eyebrow. "And you?"

"I'm all right," Jennet said easily.

"Jen"—Nancy was puzzled—"what happened to you?"

Jennet didn't want Nancy to be afraid of her and her powers. She shrugged. "Nothing." Then she thought, Powers? Not possession by a demon? This ability to feel others' pain—if it was a power to heal people, could it be evil? It was still a mystery, and yet—Jennet touched her throat, smiling in wonder.

"But why—" Nancy gestured toward the tented blanket.

"It just seemed a good idea!"

Nancy tiptoed over and peeked around the drape of the blanket. "It's like a miracle," she whispered.

Jennet sat down at An Marget's feet, and the old woman put her hand on Jennet's wet hair.

"You did well," she said, and Jennet breathed a great, good breath at the praise.

It was decided that Jemmy should stay for the night under the steamy blanket. Nancy would go home to report that all was well and come back for him tomorrow. When she went out the doorway into the rain, she turned back and kissed Jennet's cheek.

Jennet brought her quilt from the spence and slept on the floor near Jemmy's tent. During the night she roused often to check his breathing and replenish the water, clover, and honey in the kettle.

When morning came, Jemmy was as warm and wet as a stewed hen, but his cough was gone, and he was ready to rollick about, exploring the witch's cottage. After breakfast Jennet tried to keep him out of mischief, but she soon saw that An Marget was pleased to have the child there. The old woman sat in her chair and drew him against her knees to see the curious things she produced from her pocket—a fish bone wrapped in red thread, a small amber ball, a bit of wood carved with a fox's face. Jennet smiled at them as she washed the dishes. She was glad, too, that An Marget was distracted from the conjurer's book.

Nancy came soon, and An Marget told her to wait while she bottled up an infusion of red-clover medicine, which Jemmy was to sip every hour for the next two days.

Nancy said happily, "Molly says thanks, and Father says thanks. And, Jennet, you are to come to my wedding feast, the last day of May. Father says to come."

Jennet clasped Nancy's hands. "He's not angry? Should I come tonight to see him?"

The tall girl's face clouded. "No," she said slowly.

"He—takes time." Glancing at An Marget's back at the fireplace, she whispered, "He still fears for your soul."

Jennet stepped back, shaking her head. "No need."

"Well—in time—"

It was a quiet time at Chelew. The rain had stopped, and the sky was misty white. But when Jennet urged that they go outside, An Marget said it was too wet to work in the garden. She spent the day at her spinning wheel, against the coming of the man who bought thread. Then in the night Jennet heard the rain begin again, and by morning it had settled to a daylong downpour.

After breakfast, to Jennet's dismay, An Marget brought out the book and her pen. Another dark day with the manuscripts. Jennet was beginning to hate the conjurer's book. However, she hid her sigh and sat down to turning the thick yellow pages, puzzling out the words, eyes focusing suddenly on pages where mysterious words stood out in red lettering: *Stabben, Asen, Gabellum, Saheney, Noty, Enobal* . . . With the shutters drawn and the rain drumming on the thatch, it was hard to know that time passed at all. Waiting for An Marget to copy a phrase, Jennet looked longingly at the hourglass on the mantelpiece. If only it could be turned, and mark off an end to this.

Hardly noticing what she read, Jennet droned on,

" 'Experiment for'—um—'summoning spirits by writing figures—' "

"What!" An Marget exclaimed.

Jennet read it again. " 'For summoning spirits by writing figures—' " She slowed as she became alert to the words.

"Ah!" Marget cried.

Her eyes glittered, her face was transformed.

"Go on, go on!" she urged.

Jennet looked at her in fear, then down at the page. Summon spirits—her lips formed the words without sound.

"First draw the Pentacle with the star," she read, "then say these words—"

She stopped, but An Marget's look forced her to go on. She mouthed the words while the woman wrote rapidly. Then Marget snatched the book around to study the symbol on the page.

"At last! At last!" Her voice was guttural with excitement.

Forgetting Jennet, she sprang up and paced the room, head up, face exultant. She cried, "At last, Malachai!" flinging up her hands toward the magpie, who was sitting on the ladder, unsuspected by Jennet until now.

Jennet whispered, "An Marget, what—"

She didn't exist for the white witch. Margaret continued to stalk the room, eyes gleaming, and then suddenly she pulled her cloak from a peg, opened the door, and walked out into the rain. Her face was lifted, smiling, as if to a sunny sky.

Jennet hurried to the door and stood in the blowing rain as she watched An Marget go up the path to the sea cliffs. She watched the cloaked figure until it was out of sight. Then she closed the door. She looked at the dark cottage—feeble fire in the hearth, candle blown out by the draught from the door, silent magpie on the ladder. Her hands were cold. Carefully she closed the book. She lit one candle, and then another and another. She sat down on the bench by the fire and stretched out her hands to it.

No use to close the book. Or to close her eyes. The circle and the words were printed on her eyelids.

Had An Marget gone out on the cliffs to summon a spirit? Now Jennet knew whose spirit.

It can't be done—can it, God? But if it can, let it be done out there. One, two, three, four—she counted on as high as she could and started over and over again. One, two—don't think—three, four . . .

The day passed while Jennet huddled by the fire. Once she nodded and startled. *Hugh*—the thought slipped through. She went to the door and looked out through the gray rain. There'd be no sunset, but it must be nearly night. She went back to the fire—one, two—

Suddenly the door burst open, and Margaret ran in,

drenched and spattering water as she flung off her sopping cloak. Jennet started up. Was it over? The woman's face still shone with eagerness, but she could see Jennet now.

"Quick! Brush the floor, light the candles—all the candles—make a glory!"

Sweeping Jennet before her, she hurried to make the already-neat cottage shine. Placing the book on her chair, she put away the rest of the writing materials, except for the last page, which she folded into her pocket. She polished the table and spread it with a white cloth. Running back and forth, she brought out food and set it on the table, finding delicacies Jennet hadn't known about, raisins, an herb sauce, a foreign smoked fish. Jennet lit the candelabra on the mantel and another which Marget set on the table, and the cottage began to blaze with light. Malachai took alarm and flapped around the room, then disappeared up into the talfat.

"Hurry, hurry!" Marget cried as she came out of the spence.

Jennet had obeyed, swept by An Marget's urgency, but now she stopped. She stood still in the woman's path.

"An Marget, why?" she challenged. But she knew why. Her hands shook. "Please—" she begged.

Young eyes flashed in the old woman's face. "Because! Because—" Her eyes softened, and she smiled happily at Jennet. "Because," she said gently, "we are going to summon Hugh's spirit."

The room was silent, alive with light.

"No."

"Yes, Jennet. You have the power, and now we have the knowledge."

"No." She stumbled back against the door.

"Jennet—" There was pleading in the woman's voice. "I can't force you—but you need not fear evil. Hugh would never harm you." The voice became a whisper, yet it compelled. "I have waited thirty years!"

Jennet stared at the woman, who was trembling with eagerness. An Marget was mad. She was possessed by—what? Desire? Could desire be a demon? Need for love? What if it were she and Robin? Jennet pulled and twisted at her fingers, bit her lips. It was wrong, terrifying—yet . . .

An Marget seized her hands and pulled her over to the fireplace. Rapidly she strewed ashes on the clean hearth. Taking a stick, she drew a small circle around her feet and Jennet's, then a larger circle, marking it with a great star and other figures.

"God won't let you!" Jennet sobbed. "He'll laugh—I'll laugh." How could she?

Marget cried impatiently, "By my own power!"

She slipped the paper from her pocket. Holding Jennet's wrist, she began to chant the words, "Come, come, gather together, spirits of—"

Jennet stood numb with terror. She felt her mind go dim and wandering—no! *Our Father Who art in heaven . . . deliver us from evil, deliver us from evil . . . Thine is the power . . . deliver us from evil . . .*

"—*Ladodoc, Adonay!* Spirit of Hugh, appear to me!" Marget's cry ended triumphantly.

Jennet stopped breathing. She stared for a movement, strained to hear a sound. Her eyes were so wide the flames of the candles seemed to grow, filling her eyes with light. The smallest crackle of the fire was deafening.

Suddenly there was a pounding at the door. He had come.

Jennet stood rigid. Marget ran out of the circle, skirts whirling the ashes, running to the door, crying out, calling—

"Hugh! Hugh!"

She flung open the door. "Hugh!"

Oliver, Gracey Winkey's old husband, stood there.

An Marget stared at him in shock. She whirled back into the room, gazed around desperately.

"Hugh!" She flung out her arms. "Where are you?"

Jennet opened her mouth, and words came out distinctly. "Deliver us from evil. Thine is the power."

An Marget's eyes focused on Jennet. She looked at her with fury. The cords in her face were strained with fury.

"If you please, Mistress Marget—" Oliver said in a

faint, hesitant voice. "Gracey is terrible sick. She needs you."

Slowly the rage faded from An Marget's face, and her eyes seemed to blur. The old woman's shoulders slumped. Her back to the man, she looked around the room again. "Hugh?" she begged pitifully.

Marget's misery flooded Jennet. She couldn't bear it. She ran to the woman and held her close, whispering, "You know he loves you. Wherever he is, he loves you."

"Please," the little man pleaded, still in the doorway. "She's got terrible pains. Gracey's dying!"

Jennet felt the woman try to straighten her shoulders.

"Very well," Marget whispered.

But she looked dizzy, and she was breathing rapidly. Jennet led her to the chair. Putting her hands under An Marget's head scarf, she smoothed down the back of her neck. At last Marget's breathing steadied, and she heaved a deep sigh. She looked toward Oliver, beckoning him in.

"Close the door," she ordered. "The wind is blowing out the candles."

It was true. The room had lost its radiance.

Then Oliver blurted about Gracey's cramps of pain; then An Marget gathered medicines; then they set off through the night toward Kynance. Away from the sheltering hill, the wind blew in great gusts, sweeping ahead the last spits of the rain it had brought in.

In the cottage, Gracey thrashed on a bed in the corner, while Dolly and another woman tried to hold her down. When Gracey saw An Marget, she screamed out, "Oh, Mistress Marget, save me! You're the only one who can. I'm bewitched! There's a devil in my stomach, a-clawing and heaving and biting. Ohh!" She groaned and twisted.

Jennet saw a branch of ash tree fastened over the bed. Ash leaves to ward off witches.

"Nonsense!" An Marget said briskly. "Gracey Winkcy, what did you eat tonight?"

Gracey only clutched at her stomach and moaned about the Penmorvah witches, but Oliver said, "Well, there was the new cabbages, and that little pig that—" He named off a feast of bloating foods.

"Praise God!" An Marget exclaimed. "He gave me the power to heal fools!"

But she looked at Jennet, and her eyes were steady and happy. She was the White Witch of Kynance again, the woman Jennet respected. Something surged in Jennet, starting in her stomach, up through her chest. She felt a great awesome burst of laughter coming. Gracey and Dolly would never forgive her. As An Marget turned to brew up an infusion of pennyroyal and valerian, Jennet said quickly, "I'll return to Chelew."

She ran out into the windy lane, away from the

cottages, up onto the hill. Gracey and her belly and her witches . . . Jennet began to giggle . . . God sending An Marget to heal the colic . . . Yet Gracey Winkey truly needed An Marget . . . Jennet burst into laughter that rang up in the wind. It was a joke. A beautiful, wondersome joke! He'd reminded An Marget which power He had given her and which power was His alone.

And for herself—Jennet spread her hands wonderingly over her cheeks—He'd delivered her from evil.

She began to run up the hill to the moor. The wind swooped and sang around her. *Thine is the power.* Jennet flung up her arms in the wind, looking at the cloud-torn sky. Exultantly she thought, Even I can die, yet He will save me from evil!

A moon came out to light the moor, and Jennet ran over the high land toward Robin's house, to tell him to wait for her until she'd learned all she could from the white witch. She'd be no priestess of magic—and was An Marget, really?—but she could heal. And she could be a wife. Jennet laughed again softly. How Robin would tease! He had trusted all along.

HARPER TROPHY BOOKS you will enjoy reading

The Little House Books *by Laura Ingalls Wilder*

> Little House in the Big Woods
> Little House on the Prairie
> Farmer Boy
> On the Banks of Plum Creek
> By the Shores of Silver Lake
> The Long Winter
> Little Town on the Prairie
> These Happy Golden Years

Journey From Peppermint Street *by Meindert DeJong*
Look Through My Window *by Jean Little*
The Noonday Friends *by Mary Stolz*
White Witch of Kynance *by Mary Calhoun*

Harper & Row, Publishers, Inc.
49 East 33rd Street, New York, N.Y. 10016